Even Angels Cry

Even Angels Cry

Kelly M. Foster

Even Angels Cry

© Kelly M. Foster 2018

Published by
Lighthouse Christian Publishing
SAN 257-4330
5531 Dufferin Drive
Savage, Minnesota, 55378
United States of America

www.lighthousechristianpublishing.com

Chapter One

Gideon sat at his heavy, oak desk typing confidently on a small golden laptop computer. After putting the final touches on the article he was writing for the monthly newsletter, *Guardian Gazette*, he ejected the disk and placed it in an envelope, licking the flap shut.

"Being the leading authority on guarding human life certainly has its demands," he sighed and leaned back in his leather, swivel chair. The ceiling-to-floor shelves behind him were filled with books, some written by himself, containing the various logs, reports, and case studies chronicling the activities of guardian angels in human history. He had been called back to guardian duty early from his lecture circuit, during which he had spoken at nearly every angel training facility in Heaven. Hosts of eager guardian trainees and their instructors had flocked to his lectures and hung on every word.

"And so they should." Gideon brushed a speck from the shoulder of his immaculate white business suit. "After all, I've been in this business for almost 5,000 Earth years, ever since I entered training at the end of the great Demon Wars." A frantic knock on the study door interrupted his thoughts.

"Come." Gideon's authoritative voice filled the room. A young angel opened the door and the room glowed with the pure white light from outside. He was dressed in a white suit but, Gideon noticed, the style was out-dated by several decades. His pocket protector held several assorted pens and his shoes showed signs of a less than careful buffing.

"Sir Gideon, sir. Uhmm…it's almost time for the birth, and…well…" He nervously fingered his white tie.

"Ah, yes, Darius. What an excellent assistant you are becoming." Gideon rose from his chair and tucked the laptop under his arm. "Keep this up and you'll be assigned your own human being one of these centuries. The *Daily Divine* article is in the folder and the one for the *Guardian Gazette* is ready to be delivered. Send it Unblighted Parcel Service, however. I haven't regained my confidence in your material transportation skills after your disaster in trying to send my favorite suit to the cleaners." He handed the envelope containing the disk to his assistant.

"Yes, sir. I'll take care of it right away. There's a UPS office just around the corner," Darius said. "But, sir, I did eventually get your suit back."

"Yes, but only after it spent three years in purgatory. I still haven't gotten the stale smell out of it." Gideon fluffed the gold handkerchief in his breast pocket and paused by the mirror in the hallway.

"Sir, the birth. It's going to happen any moment, and you really should be there…" Darius prompted.

"Well, when you've done this kind of thing for thousands of years, you learn to take things in stride. He can't be born without me, you know. I've got all the research right here." Gideon patted the shiny gold cover of the laptop. "Little Corey Scott…brown hair, brown eyes, American, one older sister, two working parents… is about to be blessed with the epitome of guardian angel perfection." He glanced at his watch, winked at his assistant, and disappeared, leaving behind a sprinkling of gold glitter.

In the hospital delivery room, Emma Scott breathed deeply in spite of the pervasive smell of antiseptics. She had been in labor for almost eight hours and, even though she had gone through the same experience five years ago, she had not remembered the nausea and discomfort. She dutifully followed the instructions of the nurses and tried to remember what her book on childbirth had said about breathing.

In a silent sparkle, Gideon suddenly materialized in the delivery room and strolled to the mother's bedside. He took a quick look at the progress as if he had seen thousands of births before this one.

"Ah, he's almost here. A couple more minutes should do it. Come on, now, we've a deadline to meet," he said checking his watch, although neither the mother nor the medical staff was aware of his presence. He pulled his hand-held computer out of his coat pocket and scrawled a few notes on the writing pad. "And here he comes, right on schedule."

A lusty wailing filled the delivery room and the doctor handed the slippery baby to the nurse who carried him to the incubator. Gideon moved to her side to get a good look at his newest assignment. "And this is supposed to be cute, all nasty and wet?" Gideon began. "Hey, watch out!"

The nurse's hold on the squirming infant had slipped and she screamed. Gideon reacted instantly and caught the falling baby. The members of the medical staff turned toward the nurse, who was astonished to find the baby still in her arms.

"Oh," she thought quickly. "I guess I had a hiccup." She shrugged her weak excuse.

"And the score is...one for the guardian," Gideon announced to no one in particular as he licked his finger and drew a number one in the air.

Emma Scott was shuttled to the recovery room while the baby's incubator was pushed to the nursery where other newborns were either crying or sleeping. Gideon trailed behind. A young medical resident in his first pediatric internship was busy assessing one of the babies. Then he picked up Corey Scott and took him to the examining table, oblivious to the chorus of cries in the room. The nurse picked up the baby boy in the next incubator for his bath. When the resident had checked heart rate, temperature, and breathing, and had taken a drop of blood from the baby's foot, he absentmindedly placed him in the wrong incubator.

"Is there even a shred of competency left in the medical system?" Gideon exclaimed as he walked to the nurse who was drying the other baby boy. "Check the tag." He whispered the words with intense concentration.

The nurse placed the baby in Corey's incubator, tucked him under blankets and then matched the number on the arm bracelet against the number at the head of the incubator.

"Dr. Martin, you've put your baby in the wrong incubator again. Look, the Scott baby is not in his proper bed," she admonished.

"Oops." The medical student shrugged as the nurse switched the babies back.

"Oh, well that's okay," Gideon said sarcastically. "You only just about completely messed up two entire families."

Gideon peered into the incubator and tickled the baby under his chin. Little Corey closed his eyes to better concentrate on sucking his fist.

"Looks like a healthy little rug rat," Darius said over Gideon's shoulder.

Gideon startled. "Hell's horns, Darius. If you keep sneaking up on me I'm going to make you wear a bell around your neck." Gideon turned back toward the baby who picked that moment to wave a spit-covered fist in the air and hit Gideon on the nose.

"That almost looked deliberate," Darius said snatching his handkerchief from his pocket and handing it to his boss.

"Nonsense, it's just a heap of protoplasm barely controlled by a mess of neurons as unordered as a bowl of spaghetti noodles." Gideon scrubbed at his nose.

Mother and child stayed in the hospital only two days since Emma was anxious to take her newborn son home and to get some decent rest before going back to work. Besides, Rindy's babysitter had only agreed to two days.

"Dr. Smith, I've got to be back at work on Monday. Just sign us out of here. I feel fine. It's not my first baby, you know," Emma said. She worked as a corporate human resource manager and was cultivating a promotion to upper management. The doctor finally agreed and released his patients.

Robert Scott had flown in from Las Vegas where he had attended a business conference. He had missed the birth by a few hours, but had his first glimpse of his newborn son through the nursery window. He smiled proudly as he watched the baby sucking on his tiny thumb. That afternoon Robert helped his wife into the wheelchair and pushed it proudly to the exit as Emma held their baby son.

Corey fell asleep in his car seat as Robert drove his dozing wife and child home. Gideon rode in the back seat next to the baby and typed up his daily report on his laptop. The car turned onto the highway and sped across town. Suddenly, a truck in the oncoming lane blew a tire and swerved on a collision course with the Scotts' car. Robert slammed on the brakes.

"Holy Heaven!" Gideon exclaimed and a glowing ball of white light grew from his outstretched palm. He shot the light ball through the window and it deflected the course of the truck enough so that it scraped to a halt along a concrete median, barely missing the car.

"My God, we were almost killed," Robert yelled as the car slowed to a controlled speed. "Did you see that, Emma?"

"Hmm? What happened?" Emma looked around sleepily.

"That truck was coming right for us." Robert tried to get his breathing back under control. "Never mind. Go back to sleep." Robert slowly caught his breath and maneuvered the car back into the fast lane. The rear view mirror showed the driver getting out of the truck.

"Well, I can see that this will be an interesting assignment. That was a pretty close call. It looks like I will have a little talk with…let's see." He clicked on his laptop and opened a file. "Uhm, ah yes, Elina is assigned to the mother, Arelia to the daughter, and…" Gideon scrolled down. "Here it is. Hiram! No, it can't be! Hiram is back on active duty? Well, miracles do happen. Robert Scott did, after all, make it to adulthood."

A musical chime prompted Gideon to take his pager from his coat pocket. He held the device to his ear. "Speak."

"It's Darius, sir. I just wanted to remind you about the Aquarius Conference tomorrow. You're on the panel for the Planetary and Stellar Steering Committee."

"Ah, yes, thank you, Darius. Is it still at three o'clock, Celestial Standard Time? Good. I'll be there." He replaced the pager as the car slowed in front of a modest brick duplex which varied only a little from the other houses lining both sides of the street.

A group of children scampered off the sidewalk as the car pulled into the driveway. A five-year-old girl rushed out of the house. Robert parked and helped Emma out of the car.

"Oh, let me see him. He's so cute." Rindy Scott climbed into the back seat and rubbed her lips on the baby's face.

"Easy does it, young lady. Let him breathe. Rindy! What is that on your eyelids?" her father exclaimed.

"Duh! It's glitter eye shadow, Daddy. All the girls are wearing it," she insisted, rolling her eyes.

Emma bundled little Corey out of the car seat and into the house hoping for a nap after settling him in his crib. Gideon followed the family to the front steps and caught a glimpse of a shimmering glitter near the doorway.

"Well, Arelia, you're looking fit." Gideon glided over to where Rindy's guardian angel hovered a few feet off the ground, watching the homecoming.

The angel's shiny brown hair fell nearly to her waist and her white gown was attractively tied with a silver sash.

"Sir Gideon?" Arelia said in astonishment. She dropped quickly to the ground on her slippered feet and stammered. "What are…are…you…does this mean…you are assigned to…"

"Yes, dear. I still take on field assignments from time to time, you know. How has it been going with young Rindy?" Gideon asked.

"She's a sneaky little thing, growing up way too fast for a seven year old." Arelia shook her head. "She does everything she is not supposed to do and is an expert at keeping it from her parents. She has completely tuned out my promptings, and even using my still, small voice, I can't seem to get through."

"Well, remember, we are commissioned to do everything in our power to safeguard their lives and souls, not to guarantee an idealistic existence. This isn't exactly Eden, you know. We've got that issue of free will to deal with, and they do have to make their own choices. I'm sure you're doing your best with the young scamp. And I'm sure we'll be seeing a lot of each other over the next few years. Maybe I can give you some pointers."

"Oh, yes sir. I would be honored, sir. This is my first post-graduate assignment and I can use all the advice I can get."

Chapter Two

From the podium Gideon gazed out over the sea of faces. The lecture hall was packed with angels from all regions of Heaven. Those like Gideon, on active guardian duty, were easy to pick out in the crowd because they were the ones with laptop screens up, the program set on Monitor Mode displaying a screen-sized image of a human child in one stage of development or another. Gideon was used to the occasional member of his audience suddenly flicking out of sight in response to some emergency. Just last week he himself, the universally renowned Sir Gideon, had to beat a hasty and undignified retreat from the studio of the *Who's Who in Heaven* series. The live broadcast of his interview had to cut to an impromptu infomercial when his monitor showed two-year old Corey about to stick a bobby pin into an electrical outlet. It was definitely not the only crisis of Corey's first couple of years, but was one that had required immediate guardian attention. Gideon hoped that for the duration of this speech Corey would remain soundly asleep in his little toddler bed contently sucking his pacifier. The angel took one last look at his raised screen, took a deep breath and addressed his audience.

"Free will, it's just not all it's cracked up to be." He had their attention now, and deliberately took a drink of water from the glass under the podium. "This has always been one of the most obvious distinctions between God's angels and God's children. The paradox is that there is no freedom in free will. Throughout human history angels have done good deeds because they have to, and human beings have done evil deeds because they want to." He launched into a series of examples highlighting historic cases of willful disobedience to God. "We should, rather than admire human free will, pity the poor souls given this so-called gift. We angels have been given infinite gifts: power over nature, invisibility, flight, instantaneous transportation, persuasive abilities, foreknowledge of possible events, and above all else, we live in the presence of God. I propose that we are actually freer than God's children even though free will is not one of our particular gifts. And, yes, I know that some of you think that you would like to have it, but, as I have said, and I am an expert on humanity, it's just not all it's cracked up to be. It's true that we cannot choose evil over good, but this frees us from the power of evil. We are liberated from the desire to want evil or to turn our backs on our Master. His compulsion is truly our liberation!"

The words reverberated in the split second of absolute stillness of the hall before the audience broke into wild applause. "And now," Gideon said above the sound of the last straggling claps. "I have a few moments for a question or two from the audience, but let me first warn the assembly against this movement that I have been hearing about, the so-called "Free Will Front." Its misguided members, in their ignorance, are bordering on rebellion. The reason angels were not given free will is that we simply don't need it. God's grace is sufficient for us." Gideon took another sip of water and glanced at his computer screen. Young Corey was awake, but contentedly chewing on the ear of the teddy bear he had received for his second birthday.

"Sir," a young female voice piped up. "In your book, Children or Slaves, didn't you say that free will makes human beings subservient to their emotional desires? If angels had free will would we be able to do any better?"

Gideon smiled indulgently. "And you are…?"

"Valeria, sir. A harpist, sir, Symphonic Class."

"Ah, yes, how nice. I'm surprised you find the time to read with the busy schedules harpists keep to maintain the Eternal Worship. Are you sure you read the whole book? If so, you would remember that I said it would be entirely unnecessary for angels to have free will. After all, we do not forget the brightness of God's glory, which shines on us every day. Human beings, however, have no memory that their souls were formed by God's own hand, and their spirits touched by His. Memories wiped clean, they have no idea even what they should want to want. It's not that angels would use the gift better or worse, it's simply that it would make no difference. Anyone else? Yes." Gideon pointed to the waving hand.

"Sir Gideon." And angel with a sword strapped to his side stood up. "I am one of the guards of the Western Gate and I've read your book, To Will, or Not to Will."

"Yes, I recall writing that one after the Demon Battle of Terminal Expulsion, a truly glorious battle. It was the last one before the little devils realized that frontal assault on Heaven and Earth was futile and decided to become the insidious, but effective, little whisperers that they are today."

"Yes, sir, I 'm not old enough to have been in the battle, but your name is a legend among the Gate Guards. Countless legions fled screaming before your fiery sword." He stood up straighter and gripped his sword hilt.

"Yes, of course they did. Son, did you actually have a question on today's topic, or shall I direct you to the <u>Demon Chronicles</u>, my seven volume account of the Great War?"

"Well, Sir Gideon. You mentioned in the book that you believed that angels, and yourself in particular, should be given free will as a test of loyalty and devotion; that the ultimate proof of dedication to the service of the Light would be to choose light and to willfully reject evil."

Gideon hesitated. "Yes…that comment did slip through in the first edition. However," he continued quickly, "if our Lord has seen fit not to test us thus, it can only be because He already knows the outcome. We angels are incorruptible with or without free will. End of story. It would be an interesting experience, but entirely unnecessary and meaningless, as I made clear in the second edition. And, now, if you will excuse me, duty calls. Please be sure to sign up for my next lecture. I will be speaking on that great event in human life, death."

"Very enlightening speech, sir." Darius walked with his boss back to the office. "I got it on audio and video for distribution."

"Excellent. However, I want you to edit out that impertinent gate guard's question."

"The one about free will?" asked Darius.

"No, the one about bikini undergarments. Of course, the free will question, you fool," he thundered. "And confiscate all the first editions of To Will or Not to Will. It's time to bury that youthful mistake of mine."

Back in the office, Gideon sat down in his leather desk chair and propped his feet on the desk. "What's on the agenda for tomorrow?"

"Let's see." Darius whipped out his stylus and pushed some buttons on his personal organizer. "Heavenly Host at 11:00 a.m. Praise Recital right after that. Uhm…they need a substitute instructor for flight training at 1:00, and then your usual Monday, Wednesday, Friday swordsmanship class. I think that's it."

"That's fine, then. You can go for the day, while I check in on my case. He should be ready for his dinner about now," Gideon said as Darius made his way to the door. "By the way, what's the rumor down in the Nimbus?"

Darius paused and smiled at his boss's familiar mention of the Nimbus Tavern, so conveniently located in the building next to Gideon's office. There, junior angels and students hung out and compared assignments, discussed careers, and complained about bosses and professors.

"Oh, just the usual grumbling. I guess the biggest gripe is not getting enough exposure to real human beings. Most of the younger guardian trainees claim that they are ready, but the graduate students, who have finished their fieldwork, insist that they are not. I'll have your ceremonial robe ready for tomorrow morning, and have a good evening, sir."

Chapter Three

The sunbeams spilled gently from the open window in Corey's bedroom, lighting a fiery halo around his head. The five-year-old opened his eyes and smiled trying to remember what that light reminded him of when his mother bustled into the room still brushing her hair.

"Time to get up, honey. It's Sunday. Put on your church clothes. Hurry so we aren't late." She left as Corey jumped out of bed and began dressing. They were never late for church, but the family tended to cut it close sometimes. He always wore tennis shoes to church since his class played games in Sunday school.

He was halfway through his bowl of cereal when Rindy joined him at the table. She wore a tight black skirt and a leather jacket, and had spent half an hour getting her make-up to look like the models in her latest issue of *Cosmogirl Magazine*.

"Daddy back yet?" Corey asked.

"No. Mom said maybe another week." She poured a bowl of cereal. "As long as it's not before Jenny's birthday dance. I already told her I'd be there and it's really going to rock."

"Rock?" Corey asked.

"Yeah, her parents will be out of town and we're going to…never mind. Why am I telling you this anyway? Go get your hair brushed. We need to get to church early so I can sit by Jason."

"Now, children. Today's Sunday school lesson is all about angels. Who can tell me something about God's blessed servants, the angels?" Mrs. Faulk, the Sunday school teacher sat in the reading chair that she had pulled out to the center of the room. Her pre-school class of eight boys and girls sat in a semi-circle at her feet.

"Yes, Jessica?" She pointed at a little girl in a pink jumper.

"Angels are pretty and fly up high and sing." She spread her arms in a flying gesture.

"Good. Yes, Becky?"

"They sit on clouds and play the harp. And my mommy told me…"

"That's dumb," Jared interrupted. "If they sat on a cloud they would fall through. Clouds are made out of drops of water." He smiled smugly.

"Now, Jared," the teacher admonished. "You're right about what clouds are made of, but remember our class rule, everyone's ideas are welcome here. Diana, what do you think?"

"They wear flowing white robes and have golden hair and have one of those circle things over their heads."

"Very good, class. Now we will read a story about an angel that visited Earth…uh…yes, Corey? You wish to add something?"

"They wear a coat and tie and carry around a little golden computer."

Suddenly Gideon appeared at the back of the room, his laptop screen still up and a look of horrified disbelief on his face.

"Now, Corey. You're being silly, aren't you? Of course, no one in this room has ever actually seen an angel. We just use our imaginations a little, don't we? Now, the title of this story…"

"I have," Corey asserted.

"You have what, dear?" The teacher continued to flip the pages of the large book on her lap.

"Seen an angel."

That's nice, sweetie. In a book? On TV? In your…"

"I see my angel lots of times, in my bedroom, in the car, in the hospital when I got my tonsils taken out, in the playground, in church, when I'm…"

"That's enough," the teacher said sharply. "No more silliness, Corey. You have already taken up some of our story time and the other children would like to move on."

"But he's standing back there behind the toy box." Corey pointed to the back of the room and the children turned to stare.

Gideon looked down at himself. "No…invisibility is active…radiance shield is up…audio is turned on full silence. There is no way they can see me!" But he froze anyway, not daring to breathe.

"We'll have to have a little talk with your mother about your behavior in Sunday School," the teacher said sternly. "I don't believe I like your attitude. I will not allow you to further disrupt my class. Can you sit with your mouth shut and your hands folded, or do I need to send you to time out?"

Corey hung his head and popped his thumb into his mouth. As the teacher began reading the story he turned and smiled over his shoulder. Gideon felt the child's brown eyes gaze into his own.

Gideon whisked into existence in the middle of his neat study. Darius jumped up from his nap on the couch and frantically brushed the wrinkles out of his coat.

"Sir, is everything okay? I thought you were making the division report to the Holy Archangels."

"I need to sit down." Gideon fell into his desk chair and flipped up his laptop monitor. "This is serious, very serious…I've…got to do some research. Here it is, the Online Interaction Archives. Keywords: vision, presence, sight. Okay, now click to cross-reference." He began clicking furiously in the monitor's soft glow. "I need several hours of intensive work. Make sure that I am not disturbed. Oh, take an apology to the Archangels about my abrupt departure. I had a case emergency. They'll understand."

"Yes, sir," Darius agreed timidly. "Me, sir? Do you mean the actual Holy Archangels…yes, sir…Do you mean right now?"

"Go," Gideon boomed, and Darius scuttled out the door.

Corey had just tucked himself into bed and snuggled up to his teddy bear, a friend of many years despite the well-chewed ear. His mother had a business dinner and Rindy had sent him upstairs and into bed at nine o'clock. He listened for a while to the loud music from his sister's room. He could almost hear the sound of her voice on the telephone, but not quite. He dozed until he heard his mother's car in the driveway, and glanced at the digital clock his father had brought back from his trip to New York. Kneeling in bed to look outside the window, Corey stared at the moon for a long time wondering if his mother would come and check on him.

Emma kicked off her shoes at the door, set down her briefcase, and then thumped up the stairs to her bedroom. Corey sighed and sat down in bed again rearranging his blanket. He glanced around the room and froze. He hugged his teddy tightly.

Gideon had been keeping vigil that night in order to give himself time to think. He sat in the rocking chair watching the little boy and reflecting on his recent research.

"You scared me," Corey said looking directly at the rocking chair.

Gideon double-checked his concealment codes, both audio and visual.

"Who did?" he asked in the barest whisper.

"You did," the boy replied. "I didn't know you were here tonight. Sometimes when I wake up you aren't here."

"Can you see me?" Gideon ventured.

"Are you an angel? Do you have any games on your computer?" Corey got out of bed and shuffled to the rocking chair.

"You aren't supposed to be able to see me. How long have you known about me? No, wait. Let me do it." Gideon turned the computer screen toward the boy.

"I saw you before, but you never talked to me, so I thought you wanted to be a secret. I'm glad you talked to me tonight. Do you like computer games?"

"Son, I don't play games. This computer is for business. Now, I need to ascertain the extent of the security breach. What exactly have you seen me do and what do you remember?"

"Well, when I was in the hospital you held my hand, even when Mommy had to go back to the office. That time when I fell off the slide, you caught me and set me down in the sand. I think you shot a fireball or something once. And one time, I was about to see what was in those bottles under the sink, but you closed the door. I was mad about that. When that hot iron fell onto the floor, you shook my baby rattle and so I crawled to get it. And then last week, remember, I found those pill things in Rindy's purse and when you rang the doorbell she came rushing down and snatched her purse away." Corey picked up the angel's hand. "I'm glad you care about me."

"Son, uh, Corey. I guess you should know since you have probably already figured it out. I am you guardian angel and it is my job to keep you as safe as possible throughout your life without actually making decisions for you. You are not really supposed to know about me. Now, I'm going to have to requisition a memory wipe program, if they still make them, and file all kinds of reports. The red tape on this one is going to be a nightmare. Your parents have jobs, right? Well, think of it this way. You are my job. Whether I care or not has nothing to do with it. I have to guard you because that's what I do. I am a Guardian of the First Order and considered to be the best in my field. You are actually case number 303,699, and there have been quite a few little boys and girls before you." He closed the laptop with finality and started to get up.

"Can I sit on your lap?" The dark brown eyes searched his. "Please?" he asked again, the childish mouth already drooping at the corners.

The angel carefully set his computer on the floor and Corey settled into Gideon's lap, rubbing his nose on the immaculate white business suit.

"What's your name?" Corey nestled snugly.

"Gideon," came the whisper as the angel put his arms around the little boy. The moon rose in the sky, the clouds drifted outside the window, and the rocking chair creaked back and forth.

Chapter Four

"Parry one, parry two. Now lunge. That's it." Gideon's fiery sword clashed against that of the young soldier. "No! Don't retreat! Come again, from the outside this time. Good, and at ease." Gideon, dressed in full battle armor, gleaming white in the radiance of the practice chamber, lowered his flaming sword. "Not bad this time. Be a little quicker on the advance. Work on the Secondary Incursion Pattern and end with the Vindication Technique."

"Yes, Sir Gideon." The soldier, similarly arrayed, nodded and gave a crisp salute. Dismissed by Gideon's return salute, the armored angel went back to his drills and his sword circled in a complicated cadence.

"How's the battle training going, sir?" Darius appeared at Gideon's elbow.

"Rather well. This new group is quite capable and should make an excellent addition to our standing army. How's my young charge?" Gideon, with the help of Darius, began divesting himself of the armor.

"He asked for you twice, but there was no emergency," Darius smiled. "You know how ten-year-olds can be."

"He called for me? You should have informed me immediately." Gideon's eyes flashed.

"But, sir, you were in the middle of sword practice, and I just thought…well…you told me not to interrupt…and he was probably just lonely," Darius stuttered.

"That's precisely the point." Gideon allowed a brief flash of his radiant aura to surround his body. This usually served to sufficiently humble his subordinates. "As my assistant, it is your duty to keep me posted on the details of Corey's day. I'd hate to put you back on weather duty," Gideon said ominously.

"No, sir. It won't happen again. Corey made an A on his math test, wrote and essay on world peace, and walked home from school with Raven." Darius updated Gideon on the boy's activities as they left the training building. The two angels passed the entrance to the Nimbus Tavern and Darius's eyes lingered on the doorway. "Uh, sir, there is a bit of a rumor down in the Nimbus…uhm…just a silly rumor of course, but…well…"

"You know, Darius. You need to be a little more forthright in your reports. Let's see if we can't schedule you for some assertiveness training. Now, just what is this silly rumor?" Gideon paused at the door to his office building. "Out with it. I need to go to Corey."

"Well, some of the guardian-trainees suggested, in their ignorance, of course, that over the few years you have become…well…a little preoccupied with your current case." Darius stared at the white shoes of his boss. "And one of the assistant trainers, in blatant naiveté, of course, stated that perhaps your impartiality has been compromised. Isn't that ridiculous? I told him he had a lot to learn about the great Sir Gideon...uh…sir?"

As Darius was speaking, Gideon had begun to radiate a blinding brilliance and now floated above his assistant in the form of a seven-eyed seraph. "I'm sorry, sir. I didn't mean to disrupt your heavenly serenity. It's just a silly rumor that will pass. Why, you remember that rumor last year, that Friday would be blue jeans day. That one only lasted a week." Darius shielded his eyes against the glare of the seraph.

"Get back to work, Darius." A voice boomed from the seraph. "It is difficult for some to understand true greatness, but I have a job to do regardless of the trifling opinions of those less dedicated than myself." And the seraph's wings stretched out and he was gone.

Darius let out a deep sigh, held the doorknob for support, and wiped his brow with a silk handkerchief. Once inside the office, he closed the door firmly and breathed. After taking a look at the mountain of papers needing to be filed, he picked up his feather duster and lunged toward a shelf of books. After a few dusting sweeps he executed a retreat and then lunged toward another shelf.

"Well, what do you think?" Gideon floated in mid-air as Corey turned in his desk chair and squinted at the shining apparition.

"Wow, that's a great one, Gideon! What's it called?"

"A seraph." Gideon's feet touched the floor of Corey's bedroom as he transformed back into his official form and brushed a few feathers from his coat. "I only use it once in a while at the High Service and on a few other occasions as needed. I was informed that you called for me today." He pulled at his coat to straighten a wrinkle.

"Yes," Corey put down his pencil and closed his math book. He stood up and walked to the corner of the room where he had thrown his backpack. "I wanted to ask you if …you could come to a movie with me tomorrow." He pulled a folded paper from between the pages of one of the books.

"Another movie? If you need me to be there, Corey, of course I'll come. Is that the real reason you called?" Gideon answered. "What do you have there?"

Corey clutched the folded paper. "It's a weird picture that Raven gave me…and, I think it might be bad, but I'm not sure. I'm supposed to put it under my pillow and say a chant three times and then wake up in the morning with some kind of magic power. At least that's what Raven said. But I don't believe him because he is kind of mean, and he is five years older than me, so he might be trying to trick me, and…"

Gideon interrupted. "Let me see the picture." He extended his hand.

Corey hesitated. "I don't think you will like it. Maybe I'll just throw it away. I shouldn't have even told you."

"Show me the picture, Corey. It might be important."

Corey slowly unfolded the paper and held it up. Gideon stepped back and instinctively reached for the sword that was no longer at his side. A shadow seemed to pass before his eyes as he beheld a goat's head outlined with an inverted pentagram drawn in black marker.

"Tear it up, Corey," Gideon whispered. "It is a sign of evil. I fought in the front lines for seven centuries against the hideous legions which marched under that banner." Corey stared at the symbol with wide eyes and carefully began to tear it up.

"Throw it away and think no more about it. It does not give power, but it has power to make you a slave in the service of evil. You know I am right. You felt its wrongness. You didn't need me to tell you that."

The tiny pieces of paper lay in the trashcan and Corey slumped on the edge of his bed. "I know, Gideon. I knew it was wrong even when I got it from Raven. But it would be nice to be powerful like you. You can do all kinds of things, like throwing fireballs, and casting lightning, and flaming up your sword, and turning yourself into cool things. And I can't do anything neat like that. If I had your kind of power, I'd make tons of money so Mom and Dad wouldn't have to work all the time, and I'd make Rindy see that her new boyfriend is a real jerk, and I'd make Adair notice me, and I'd make Trent believe in God, and…"

Gideon sat on the edge of the bed and put his arm around the boy's shoulders. "Corey, haven't I taught you anything about free will? Remember when you were five years old and you wanted me to show myself to your Sunday school teacher so that she would stop teasing you? She has a right to her own beliefs and my appearance might have caused her to change those beliefs. Remember when you were seven and wanted me to cross some wires on your father's car so that he wouldn't leave for Washington? That would have been interfering with his choice to go. Everyone has to make their own decisions, and even guardian angels are prohibited from directing human choice."

"But, Gideon, you give me advice all the time, and I always take it. And didn't you say that you'd have a talk with Mom's guardian angel, Elina, for her to whisper in Mom's ear whenever she forgets to hug me before leaving for the office?" Corey asked.

"That's not the same thing. Guardians can whisper, argue, and even shout, but when a human makes a choice, that's it. Our hands are tied. We get a lot more action when our humans are very young. The actions of children are not really choices. When a baby tries to drink drain cleaner, it's not because of a conscious decision, but an instinct to explore something new. Do you see the difference between simple curiosity and a willful decision? If you decided to sleep with that abominable symbol under your pillow, even knowing it was wrong, I could not, and would not, prevent it."

"I don't want free will, Gideon. I might do something wrong."

"Don't ever say that! Free will is the greatest gift given to human beings. It allows you to choose good even in the face of evil. Every human being makes good and bad choices. God is more pleased by the sheep that have strayed and returned than the ones who never left the fold. Do you understand?"

"I think so. But do you ever see God?" Corey asked shyly. "It would be better if people could see Him and then it would be easier to choose good."

"Ah, but if you saw Him in all His glory, then you would have no choice but to believe. Your free will would be compromised. And yes," Gideon said rising, "as an angel of considerable rank, I come into His radiant presence quite often as part of the Heavenly Host. Some day you will see Him, too. But, now, I believe you have Math homework to finish. I'll check in on you tomorrow and, Corey, stay away from Raven."

Gideon allowed Darius to help him adjust the folds of his dress robe as he readied himself for his shift in the everlasting court, arrayed in worship since the dawn of infinity. This was to be a court of judgment, Gideon discovered, after checking the schedule. He walked slowly through the courtyard with the other angels on his shift and composed himself to serenity. The huge white pillars that held aloft the cathedral ceiling gleamed and the sparkling white steps beckoned ever upward to the thrones. As Gideon took his place, the air was infused with the clear voices of the choir, which rose in adoration as the harp players joined the crystalline music.

In Gideon's office Darius, as instructed, kept vigil in front of the computer monitor, but his eyes kept straying to the pages of a book. <u>Fundamentals of Transformation</u> lay open on his lap. On the monitor Corey tossed under his covers. The boy's gaze strayed to the trashcan and he got out of bed. After several minutes of searching he deposited a handful of paper bits on his blanket and knelt by the bed. Darius glanced up and tried to make out the picture puzzle that Corey was piecing together, but after a half hour of work, the boy gave an expression of annoyance, scooped up the bits of paper, and threw them in the trashcan. His sleep was restless that night.

Chapter Five

"So, did you try out the power spell?" Trent asked Corey. The junior high school girls' volleyball game they were watching had halted while the referees argued.

"Yeah, of course, I did. But it didn't work."

"Me, neither. But it was kind of fun. Hey, look, is that your sister over there making out on the bleachers?"

Corey looked across the court and saw Rindy in a face lock with her current boyfriend. Whatever his name was.

"Looks like she's going to suck his face off," Trent said. "Maybe I'd better spend more time at your house."

"That's just gross, Trent. Anyway she's graduating from high school next year. Watch the game." Corey shoved Trent's shoulder.

"Okay, okay. Don't be so defensive. Look, Adair's in the next play. Ohh yeah, and so is Candie. She's hot! The first thing I'd do with magic power is to get Candie alone in my bedroom. Sweet! Look at her tight buns."

"Uhh, yeah, sure. Like you know what to do in bed."

"Oh, ye of little faith. Know you not that man cannot live on bed alone? There's also the couch and the back seat of my car."

"Oh, yeah. You mean the car you don't have yet. Well, gosh, only three years to go. Besides, Candie doesn't even like you. And Adair thinks I'm a fly on the ceiling. Not much potential to score there. Anyway I thought your parents wouldn't let you date yet."

"My philosophy is that what my parents don't know won't hurt them. A little knowledge can be a dangerous thing." Trent and Corey rose with the crowd that cheered when the home team scored a point.

"Okay, so what's our great plan to get Candie and Adair to come to their senses?" Corey sneaked a look over his shoulder to where Gideon sat at the top of the bleachers talking to the air and oblivious to the game below.

"Adair and Candie are best friends, right? Well, Candie is sleeping over at Adair's house tonight so we can arrange to have a little technical problem with our bikes right outside Adair's house. We'll ask to use their phone."

"Oh, right. Like they're going to believe that," Corey scoffed.

"It doesn't matter if they believe it. We just need to create a memorable event. It's just a first step, you know. Unless you have any better suggestions."

"Are those girls' legs longer than they're supposed to be?" Gideon remarked. He and Nathan were sitting on the top row of the bleachers.

"Are you just now noticing the legs? You need to get out of the office more. Biologically speaking, I think they're about the usual length, but the shorts are considerably shorter than back in the seventeenth century when you were last out in the field," Nathan said. "Now we were discussing the little problem of your recent publicity."

"Oh, right," Gideon turned back to Nathan. "It seems that someone has been leaking details of my work with Corey to the tabloids. I've been careful to write my official reports as vaguely as possible, but somehow my more unconventional activities have found their way into print, sensationalized to the hilt, of course. For example, last week the *Heavenly Inquirer,* published an article titled 'Gifts of the Spirit: Not Just for God Anymore.' All I did was give Corey a little present on his thirteenth birthday. Just a little practice sword, non-flaming, of course."

"Why would anyone bother going to the tabloids? There's no profit in it, and besides, the tabs are only circulated in the outer districts where angels are bored silly from continually guarding the gates from attacks which haven't occurred for centuries."

"Well, one has to be constantly on guard about one's reputation. I just wonder who's been shirking their duties long enough to even have time to spy on me," Gideon said.

"Don't look at me. I've been putting in overtime hours with Trent for the last five years. But I wouldn't worry about it if I were you. You obsess too much. I'm going to head back to the office to finish a couple of reports. You going to stay here for a while?"

"No, I have to get back for a conference with a student. Seems he thinks he can graduate without writing a decent research paper, imagine that!" Gideon and Nathan vanished into the bright lights of the gymnasium.

"Okay, so you know the game plan, right?" Trent said. "Six o'clock in front of Adair's house." Trent and Corey got up to leave with the rest of the crowd. The home team had won the first game of the season, and family members were pouring onto the court to congratulate the players.

Corey rode his bike in the descending twilight to Adair's neighborhood. Two-storey mansions lined the street and Corey thought of his modest three-bedroom duplex. Both cars were parked in the driveway, so he knew that Adair and her parents must be back from the game. He waited by a tree for maybe ten minutes until Trent pedaled up on his bike.

"Okay, let's do it. I've only got an hour to be home or else my parents will ground me again."

They walked up to the door and rang the bell. Adair's mother answered.

"Good evening, Mrs. Matthews-Green," Trent began. "We're sorry to bother you, but would you mind if we used your phone? Bicycle problems."

Corey nodded and pointed to the two bikes lying in the yard.

"Corey, is that you?"

"Yes, ma'am. And this is my friend, Trent."

"Well, I haven't seen you since you and Adair were in that cute Sunday school play when you were little. Come on in, boys. Adair," she called. "Come show your friends where the phone is."

"Score," Trent whispered behind Mrs. Matthews-Green's back. "Ask and you will deceive, so that your ploy may be complete."

"You were awesome in the game tonight, Adair," Corey said sipping the lemonade Adair had poured for him. Trent had started sulking ever since he had learned that Candie was taking a long shower.

"Why, thanks, Corey. I haven't seen you in a long time. Do you remember that stupid play we were in together? You were a shepherd, and I had to be a cow instead of Mary."

"Uh, yeah. I thought you were a great cow though. I mean you would have been a great Mary, too. So, what classes are you taking?" Corey gulped some lemonade.

"Well, I got into the high school fashion design elective. That's what I'm going to go into as a career. Some day I'll own my own design corporation. The other courses are just the usual boring stuff, except volleyball, of course. What are you planning on as a career, Corey?"

"Not sure yet, but something that involves travel. I want to see all the historic places on earth, the sites of all the world's major events. Maybe I should be a photographer or a travel journalist. But I've got a lot of time to think about it and my whole life to spend traveling," Corey said.

"Oh, yeah, me too. I mean I want to travel. Shopping in Paris, lunch in Venice, nightlife in Madrid. That's the life for me. What about you, Trent? Going to be a preacher like your dad?"

"Hell, no," Trent barked. "I don't want anything to do with religion and all that crap about salvation." He slammed his glass on the table and Corey and Adair froze. "Hey, chill out," Trent laughed. "Just kidding. Maybe I will be a preacher. What do you think about this sermon?" Trent stood up, threw back his head and spoke in a deep, authoritative voice. "The cages within is death, but the free gift of God is eternal strife. But only if your faith is the size of a flustered weed, for with God all things are impossible."

Adair burst into laughter. "That was excellent, Trent."

Corey turned his smile into a sip of lemonade.

"Thank you, my child." He sat down again. "Now, where the hell is Candie? How can anyone take that long in the shower?"

"Well, she's shaving her legs, you know," Adair explained collecting the empty lemonade glasses. "I thought you guys called for a ride home. It's 8 o'clock already."

"Crap, we've gotta go. Come on Corey. I guess our ride isn't coming, but I'd better get home before my parents notice that I'm past curfew." Trent headed toward the door. "Tell Candie I'm sorry I missed her, but I was thinking about her in the shower the whole time," he leered.

"Uh, yeah, sure I will. You guys can leave your bikes on the lawn until tomorrow if you want to. Maybe I'll see you in school, Corey." Adair closed the door and the boys walked to their bikes.

"Well, that was successful," Corey mused. "I mean for me. Bad luck for you, but there's always next time, right?

Trent rode off down the street, standing up on his pedals to make faster time. Corey turned his bike in the opposite direction and headed home wondering if it was too late to get into the fashion design elective.

Chapter Six

"Are you still brooding about that silly article, Gideon?" Corey sat at a picnic table at the park trying to read the new novel assigned by his eighth grade English teacher. Gideon sat on the opposite bench pouring over a newspaper. "And you thought I was becoming obsessive with World of Warcraft, a mere computer game."

Gideon had insisted that Corey get out of the house for some fresh air after three afternoons straight of planning battle strategies against orc armies. "I just don't know how these idiots can warp information so outrageously. Listen to this headline, "A Match Made in Heaven?" It starts, 'Sir Gideon, former master of arms at Outpost Omega and former member of the Gamma Omicron Delta fraternity'...I mean, come on. I only took that position at Omega because I knew that the dean of the Guardian Graduate School had served there and I wanted to be sure he noticed my application. I resigned that position within a few weeks. It was practically in the Nether Reaches. And as for that fraternity, well, we're talking centuries ago. Notice that the article doesn't mention my tenured professorship at the University of Heaven, that I'm a published and widely read author, the chairangel of the Guardianship Oversight Committee, a decorated general from the Demon Wars, and a three time swordsmanship gold medal winner at the Celestial Games. They highlight the least important, but most controversial aspects of my past, while conveniently avoiding all of the contributions I've made and positions I now hold."

"Okay, okay, I didn't mean to get you all fired up. It's just a tabloid. You said nobody reads them anyway. Didn't they run an article last week about a Bigfoot sighting out in the Nimbostratus? So what's the big deal about this one?" Corey put his bookmark at the beginning of chapter ten.

"The big deal is that someone is feeding them information. The article goes on to suggest that I am practicing matchmaking, which everyone knows is in direct violation of the Guardian Code. It says that I seem to have given insider information to a human male, which, I assume, would be you, concerning the favorite flower of a human female. Well, you would have found that out anyway. So where's the scandal?" Gideon crumpled the newspaper into a ball and tossed it into a nearby trashcan.

"Oh, yeah, I forgot about that. Adair sure liked that jasmine flower I left on her desk. We sat together at lunch that day," Corey smiled wistfully. "But that can't be counted as matchmaking. Adair and I are still just friends. She says she can't date until she's fifteen anyway. You've got to get your mind off all the rumors. What about a little sword match? I've been practicing. Here, I can use this stick." Corey picked up a sturdy stick about four feet long and swept it through the air.

"You're right. Why should I be concerned with the opinions of those less enlightened than I am? En garde." Gideon picked up a nearby stick slightly longer than Corey's.

The two began sword sparring, parrying, and lunging around the table, a tree, and a trash can. Corey dutifully picked up his stick sword each time he was disarmed and attacked with renewed enthusiasm. The final engagement ended with Corey's sword flying through the air to become stuck in the branches overhead.

"Well done, Zorro," Trent emerged from behind the tree clapping. "I've never seen anyone do a sword kata and drop their sword so many times. You need a lot more practice."

"Trent, I didn't see you there. I was just practicing by myself here in the park, alone," Corey gasped, trying to catch his breath.

"Obviously," Trent rolled his eyes. "With skill like yours it's no wonder you come way out here; so no one sees you flailing about and so you don't kill any innocent bystanders." He looked up at the branches. "Time to beat that into a ploughshare. Hey, kid, breathe. You look pale as a ghost. You're not going to pass out are you?"

"I'm okay, just a bit winded. I should work out more," Corey puffed.

"Your reason you shall keep if you faint not. You've never been much of an athlete, but looks to me like you're getting worse. " Trent walked over to the picnic table and picked up Corey's book. "Probably studying too much. I didn't bother reading this one. The Cliff Notes was just as good. In wisdom there is grief and he who increases knowledge should increase it tomorrow."

"You do know, don't you, that your scripture quotation skills are the pits. Do you have to corrupt everything from the Bible?" Corey perched on the table, using the bench as a footrest.

"For a church boy, you don't know much. I bet you've never read the Gospel according to Trent. It's the fifth book of the New Testament and the only one worth anything. My parents have quoted verses as often as they breathe for my entire life. They think that something will sink in and maybe someday I'll be a good person. Well, it sank in all right, right to the bottom of the cesspool."

"Trent, there is a God," Corey said quietly.

"Oh, there is...oh my gosh...whatever will I do? And I've been such a bad boy."

"Hey, He exists whether you believe in Him or not. And He loves you and me and everyone in the world."

"Yeah, right. Look, if you can give me just one honest answer, then I'll believe and reform my evil ways. Why would God love us?"

"He loves us because...well, He just does...because he's God...it's His nature..." Corey started.

"I thought so. That's not an answer and it's not a reason. I'll keep on being an atheist." Trent started to leave.

"Wait, what do you believe in?" Corey asked.

"Just the truth. There is no God. Believe it, Corey. The truth shall set you free."

"That didn't go so well, Gideon." Corey said.

"You did your best. That was definitely a tough one. Well, we'd better be getting you back home. I've got to get ready for a staff development retreat sponsored by the university. UHP requires us to attend these silly things at least once a century. Tedious for me, but it allows the younger faculty members to rub elbows with the full professors and get advice on their research projects."

"Gideon," Cory said picking up his book and key ring. "What is the answer? Why does God love us? I can't imagine why he would, but I've always taken it for granted."

"Well, it's because He went to a lot of trouble for you, and all of humanity." Corey and Gideon started walking toward the park exit. "You can't even begin to imagine what He endured for your salvation. So, that kind of makes human beings pretty valuable. Like if you had a quarter and accidentally dropped it down a hole. Then while you were reaching into the hole you fell in. You fell a thousand miles through a forest that flayed your skin off. Then you ended up caught in the branches of a tree without food or water until you died. Then you kept falling through another thousand miles of fire and ended up in the middle of a lake of lava. There you found your quarter floating on the surface and you grabbed it. After walking a thousand years to get back home, just you and your quarter, you finally made it and saw a vending machine. Would you spend that quarter for a drink?"

"Hell, no. Not after all that."

"So the quarter had become valuable to you; worth much more than twenty-five cents, right? But had the quarter changed any from the ordeal or had you changed?"

"Okay, I see why we're valuable and loved now. But what made God reach into that hole in the first place?"

"Ah, our entire Philosophy Department has been debating that for eternity. Every few centuries the department announces that they are close to solving the puzzle, but then they say they need more time and nothing is ever published. They're a bit obsessive that way. I guess some people just don't like mysteries."

Chapter Seven

"Well, Hiram. I see that you do bother to show up once in a while." Gideon leaned against the kitchen counter while Corey went upstairs to brush his teeth. Hiram reached breathlessly for the back of a kitchen chair. He wore a white jogging suit and tennis shoes.

"Gideon," he breathed. "I see you're still hanging over your case like a brain dead vulture." Hiram struggled to catch his breath.

"It's nice to see you, too. Now, let me guess. Either you have forgotten your instantaneous transport code, or you are training for the Olympics," Gideon smiled condescendingly.

"You are just too perceptive," Hiram said sarcastically. "Actually, I'm going to be issued a new code word next week, but have to use good old leg power until then. I think I might actually be getting into shape." He patted his abdomen. "My case hasn't left yet has he? Thank God! He is catching a plane to New York and I didn't fancy a marathon to the airport."

"Another trip? Have you been working on his sense of responsibility to family?"

"Of course," Hiram said in an injured tone. "Whatever I say about commitment to family he interprets as needing to work harder, take more trips, and make more money for his family. He may not be the interacting type, but he's very dedicated."

"Well, try harder. My Corey is growing up without him. He just turned fourteen and only his sister and her biker boyfriend were around to take him out for a hamburger and a milk shake. I'm about to walk him to school, but just out of curiosity, you did check with FutureLine about the status of Mr. Scott's flight, didn't you?"

"I always check out the flights. According to FutureLine this one is shrouded, I have to admit. But the man's been on shrouded flights before, and he wouldn't listen anyway if I suggested he postpone the trip or take another plane. He would never change business plans. I should know," Hiram nodded.

"Well," Gideon shrugged. "He's your case."

"That he is. And just out of curiosity, doesn't the great Gideon have other things to do than walk a teenage kid to school?"

Gideon glared at the other angel. "It's different when they can see you. Corey wants me to be there and enjoys my company. Here comes Robert. Now get on with your job."

Hiram followed Robert out the front door but called back over his shoulder, "He's just a human being. You don't need to live his life."

Gideon began to frame an appropriately chastising remark, but Corey and his mother came down the stairs.

Her movements were almost robotic as she packed papers in her briefcase. After almost twenty years with the same company, she had thought to be secure in the ranks of upper management by this time, but had been bypassed for promotion five times already.

"Working late tonight, Mom?" Corey asked putting a book in his backpack.

"Yes, honey. I've got a meeting with one of the sales managers. Are you okay? How's school? It seems like I never get to see you anymore." She closed her briefcase and looked up.

"Everything's cool, Mom. Don't worry about me. I'm great," Corey forced an extra degree of cheerfulness in his voice.

"That's nice, dear. You are still walking to and from school with some of your buddies, aren't you? It's not a safe neighborhood."

"Yes, Mom. I'm always with someone." He flashed a smile in Gideon's direction. "Well, got to run. Have a nice day." He and Gideon left the house.

"Brain dead vulture?" Gideon mumbled, lost in his own thoughts as he accompanied Corey on his walk to school.

"You're awfully preoccupied," Corey said. "What's up in Heaven?"

"Oh, the usual sublime serenity, with a healthy dose of peace." Gideon broke his musing and answered. "What's up with you?"

"Well, I got Trent to ask Adair if she'd go out with me. He's supposed to give me her answer today after school. And I've got a geography test today. I'll ace it, of course. Mrs. Johnson liked my essay on capital punishment. I got an A. Report cards come out today. Oh, and you don't need to meet me after school. Me and the guys are going to hang out at Trent's house today." Corey picked up the pace and walked on in silence.

Gideon glided gracefully at the boy's side occasionally sneaking glances at his expressionless face. "Is there anything wrong, Corey? You know you can tell me anything."

"Wrong? Of course not, Gideon," Corey forced a laugh. "It's just…well, never mind…it's a human thing." The school parking lot came into view. "I'll check you later. Gotta run." Corey waved and ran the rest of the way just as the first bell began to ring. He had seven minutes to get his breathing back under control before the tardy bell rang.

"Hey, Cor." Trent yelled and Corey ran to catch up. They opened their lockers, which were on the same wall, and began hauling out books. "Mommy lets you walk to school alone?"

"Well, of course. She lets me do anything I want. We still meeting at your house after school?" Corey asked.

"Yep. My parents won't be home until six and the whole gang is going to be there, including Raven." Trent slammed his locker.

"Raven's coming?" Corey looked up.

"What's the matter with you? Can't handle it? Feel free to wimp out if you want. Let your light whine." Corey and Trent negotiated the crowded hallway and slipped into their first class.

Gideon sipped a steaming mug of tea, and the leather of his desk chair squeaked as he reclined. He checked his watch and then set down the mug as a knock sounded at the door.

"Enter," Gideon stood up and watched as an angel came in the door brushing off specks of glittery light onto the study floor.

"A bit of precipitation today," the angel apologized. "You wished to see me, Gideon?"

"Yes, Nathan. I appreciate your promptness. Please have a seat." Gideon sat and gestured to a chair that Nathan pulled up in front of the great desk. "It's been a while since we talked business. Corey and Trent are still spending a good deal of time with each other. Please, have a cup of tea." A cup appeared in Nathan's hand.

"Yes, that's true. He and Trent seem to have developed quite a friendship. And by the way, you are doing an excellent job on your human being. He has a good soul and an ample share of common sense. Of course, I'm doing my best with mine. However, in spite of my best efforts, he declared himself an atheist as soon as he knew the meaning of the word. My case is a bit harder stuff to work with than yours. It would help greatly if Trent could actually see me." Nathan laughed and took a sip of tea.

"Are you, by chance, saying that my Corey is turning out well because he is naturally good or is merely easier to work with? Are you implying that I've got a cushy job just because the boy is highly perceptive?" Gideon began to glow around the edges.

"Oh, calm down, Gideon. If you turn yourself into a seraph, I'll have to join the party as a cherub or something. And a naked, winged baby right here in your office might not be a pretty sight."

Gideon laughed and relaxed. "No, I'd rather not see your cherubic impression right now. Once was enough!"

"We go back a long way, Gideon, right to the beginning of the Guardian Order. You were my mentor for many centuries, and so I need to ask if perhaps you are spending a little too much energy on this case of yours."

"I appreciate your concern, Nathan. But this case happens to interest me, and I haven't had such an interesting assignment in countless human lifetimes." He drank the last swallow from his mug and then refilled it with a nod of his head. "Corey is one of the best human souls I have had the pleasure to work with, and, yes, I do take some credit for his righteousness. I interact with him constantly to insure that this one doesn't go astray. I have high hopes for presenting him for sanctification at his Judgment," Gideon said.

"Sounds like you are trying to make a saint, Gideon. No, no, hear me out. The kid's only fourteen. A lot could happen in a lifetime. Besides you always told me not to get personally involved, not to congratulate myself halfway through the job, and to remember that they are only human," Nathan said.

"I hope you also keep in mind," Gideon answered, "that I never asked for special privileges in my assignments. In spite of several memos, I have not yet been informed as to the reason Corey can see me, nor the status of the memory wipe program I requested so many years ago. Certainly you are not going to suggest that a mistake of some kind has been made."

"The thought never crossed my mind, Sir Gideon. Can I be of further service to you?" Nathan set his mug on the desk.

"Just keep an eye on your case if he is going to be associating with Corey. If you do your job well, he won't be a negative influence on my boy. Now, good day, Nathan, and thank you for coming." Gideon stood up and took Nathan's hand.

"Always a pleasure," Nathan said.

Chapter Eight

"That's my point," Trent called out. "It tipped the edge." He and Corey had been playing ping-pong in the basement of Trent's house for half an hour. Ben and Logan had already arrived and were playing foosball.

"Okay, you win this time." Corey put his paddle away. "When are the others getting here?"

"They'll be here soon. Have patience. To everything there is a treason, and a time for every purpose under Raven." Trent smiled maliciously.

As if in response, the doorbell rang and Trent dashed up the stairs. He returned followed by four teenage boys, Tom and Billy, brothers, and their friend, Joey, who had only been to one previous meeting. An older boy followed them down the basement stairs like a shadow.

"All right," came the older boy's scratchy voice. "Let's get this meeting together. Lock the door, Tom. Get the altar set up, Trent. Billy, you get ready to kill the lights." The boys hurried to obey. Raven's small bright eyes darted around the room and his jet-black hair was pulled back and tied at the nape of his neck.

Trent took a black cloth from a plastic bag, and Tom dragged a storage trunk to the center of the room. Joey lit the black candle and set it on top of the cloth-covered trunk. The boys stood back and looked at Raven who had not moved from the foot of the stairs, but stood with arms folded as he surveyed the group before him. A heavy darkness crept into the air and he nodded for the lights to dim.

"What's going on, Trent?" Corey breathed as the room became dark. "This is creepy."

"Shut up, Cor. Just watch and keep your mouth shut. It's time to grow up." Trent dragged Corey by the arm to the middle of the room.

"Gather around the dark altar, lit only by the elemental forces of fire, our lord's own essence." Raven's voice was disembodied in the darkness and the boys gathered around the altar. Raven's heavy steps could be heard until his form appeared in the flickering circle of candlelight. He raised both hands toward the ceiling, palms up, and groaned deeply. Corey watched as Raven's body suddenly tensed and he fell on his knees at the altar and lowered his hands, palms together, to stop a foot above the candle. He began swaying in a hypnotic rhythm.

Corey nudged Trent's arm, but Trent hit him lightly in the side and hissed, "Just watch. You're going to miss it."

Raven had begun a wordless chant and slowly separated his palms. A glow began to form in the space between his hands, and the chant became faster. The seven boys were statues, hardly daring even to breathe as

Raven placed his hands on the altar and a ball of glowing light remained floating in the air.

"The energy has been gathered. The petition has been uttered. The way has been opened. Come, lord, appear to your servants, that all may know the power of the Lord of Darkness." Raven's voice rose in volume and pitch as he spoke this last word. Suddenly the glowing ball began to shimmer and elongate.

Corey could not take his eyes from the apparition and saw a grotesque outline of a man's face begin to appear. One of the boys fell on his knees, and the others looked like flat manikins, suspended in both time and space. The mouth of the face was a gaping black hole that opened and closed. The eyes were red orbs floating in black sockets.

"Speak, Master of Evil. We await your command." Raven bowed his head. The face contorted in a grimace and its image began to deform. Suddenly, the face was gone and the glow above the altar disappeared. A noxious smoke formed in its place and the smell of rotten meat permeated the air.

"Unbelievers!" Raven hissed as he glared at the boys clustered around the altar. "Get the lights. I have no more energy for another try. Someone here doesn't believe." He looked at each of the boys in turn. "You have no idea how much power can be offered to you if you believe and embrace the darkness. We'll meet again next week, my place, but leave your childish doubts behind and come prepared to sample your first taste of power."

Corey walked home alone in the lengthening shadows. The weight of his backpack seemed to be dragging him back and the air was humid and oppressive.

He tried to keep his mind on the events of the school day and away from what had just occurred in Trent's basement.

The front door was locked as usual, and Corey pulled the key ring from inside his shirt where he wore it on a long shoestring. Letting himself in and dropping his backpack by the door, he sank wearily onto the living room couch.

Corey awoke in darkness, huddled on the couch. The sun had long since set and the house was still and lifeless.

"Mom, Rindy?" he called.

He looked at his watch, and then looked again. It can't be nine o'clock. Where was everybody? He turned on the lamp, got up from the couch, and began turning on all the downstairs lights. There were no messages on the answering machine and no notes stuck to the refrigerator. Neither his mother's nor Rindy's car was in the driveway.

Corey jerked in alarm as the phone suddenly rang.

"Mom? Where are you? I thought you were going to be home at six."

"Corey, honey," his mother's voice cracked. "I'm at the airport. There has been an accident…I…is Rindy home?"

"Her car's not here. I guess she's working late at the bowling alley. What's wrong, Mom? What kind of accident? Are you okay?"

"Your father's plane has crashed," his mother sobbed. "We don't know who the survivors are yet. I'm waiting for the airline officials to make an announcement. Corey…Corey… say something."

"I'm here, Mom," his voice trembled.

"Just stay by the phone, sweetheart. I'll call as soon as I know something. Lock the door."

Corey sat down on the couch and put his head in his hands. "Gideon?" he called.

"I'm here, son." The angel appeared on the couch next to the boy.

"Oh, Gideon…my father…" he started.

"I know. You have to be strong. This is a turning point in your life." He put a hand on the boy's arm.

"I have to know…is he…did Dad…?"

Gideon sighed heavily. "Yes, he is dead." And he felt the heaving of the boy's young shoulders. As he drew the boy toward him he recalled the countless times when he had held this young soul in his arms to give comfort, to console, to calm. Slowly Corey mastered his emotions and drew a shaky breath.

"It's Hiram's fault. What kind of messed up guardian angel is he anyway? He should have protected him."

"There's no one to blame, Corey. Although Hiram and I tend to disagree on certain protocol interpretations, not to mention that he only got into the guardian training program because of a glitch in the database, his reports have all been in order and are reviewed regularly by the Novice Oversight Committee. He conducted himself in accordance with guardian regulations and is, as I am, bound by rules of non-interference. We're not omniscient, you know. Human fate unfolds with as much novelty for us as it does for mortals. No one can read the end of the book first. And anyway, everyone dies eventually."

"Why, Gideon?" Cory's tears began again.

"Why do human beings die? From the moment of birth you are living on borrowed time. The only door back to eternal light is through death. I thought I taught you that," Gideon said gently.

"Why did it have to happen to Dad? Why is this happening in my life? Why did I have to make it happen?"

"Son, first of all, you do not have the power to make an event like this happen. As to why it happened to your dad at this particular time, I'm afraid that even angels don't have that kind of knowledge. Even with the best of guardian angel diligence, death happens. You certainly can't blame yourself."

"Well, you don't know, Gideon," Corey shouted. "I thought you kept an eye on me. I thought all the important events in my life were recorded by your little computer. Where were you this afternoon that you missed what I did at Trent's house?" Corey stood up suddenly and ran up the stairs.

Gideon sat still a few moments and then he opened his laptop on the coffee table. Clicking on the day's monitor folder he stared at the recording on the screen. The images of terrified boys, a glowing light and a mockery of a human face caused Gideon to close his eyes, turn away, and shut down the computer.

"Corey?" The boy lay on his bed under the covers, and Gideon shook his shoulder.

"Go away! Why are you still here when you know what I did?" Corey turned to face the wall.

"Yes, I know, but what I don't know is why you didn't leave, or call for me. You know I would have come, even into a room filled with evil. God knows I've come in closer contact with evil than that little ritual. But, you know why you didn't call, don't you?"

"I guess...I didn't want you there...because, if you were there, I would have had the sense to leave. And...I didn't want to leave."

"Right. I can only guide and counsel, not make your decisions. But, Corey, that little light show was not real power. I was just a stunt to impress kids like you and get you to believe that great powers can be yours if you serve evil. You were only an observer and didn't actively participate. To look at evil does not make one evil. Think of the demon hordes I have seen, and I assure you, they reeked of evil. You have done nothing, in any way, to cause the plane crash." Gideon sat down on the bedside and Corey moved over to make room.

"I loved my dad, Gideon." Corey turned over. "You know I loved him. But, you are more like a father to me. I love you."

"And I you, Corey." He bent to return the hug. "We'll get through this together."

"I won't do it again. I promise."

Chapter Nine

"Dust to dust, ashes to ashes," the pastor intoned. "May the Lord in His mercy, accept the soul of our departed friend. Amen."

"Amen," the congregation echoed. Emma, Corey, and Rindy sat on the front pew of the church, which was filled with friends and family of Robert Scott. Emma held a handkerchief to her eyes and bowed her head in grief. Corey chewed his fingernails. Rindy sat stiffly erect, her dark hair hanging straight to the shoulders of her black leather jacket. She had perfected the gothic look with white foundation, black lipstick, and heavy eyeliner.

The limousine ride to the cemetery was deathly quiet as the Scott family members stared out of their respective windows. It was a smaller group that gathered around the rectangular opening in the earth and watched as the coffin slowly descended. Emma began to cry and Corey took her hand. The sympathizers drifted away and the dirt piled higher in the grave.

"Let's go home, Mom. Want Rindy to drive?" Corey said, taking his mother's hand and leading her toward the car. Rindy walked silently behind them but looked up expectantly at the sound of a motorcycle.

"No, Rindy," Corey admonished. "You need to be home for Mom. This isn't the time to run off." He helped his mother to the car.

The rider of the motorcycle stopped beside the cemetery fence and took off his helmet. It was Rindy's boyfriend, Dane.

"You stay with Mom. I've got to go. Maybe we just can't all be as perfect as you." Rindy hopped on the back of the bike and held onto Dane's waist as he roared out onto the road.

"What did I do wrong, Corey?" Emma broke the awkward silence as she drove slowly through the back roads to their neighborhood. "My husband is gone. My daughter has turned away from me. My career has hit a brick wall. Only you are left to me."

"No, not only me, Mom. There's God, too."

Emma smiled at her son. "I wish I had your faith."

Gideon scanned the board just inside the entrance to Harmony Hall, one of the largest and newest buildings in the City of God and a hallmark of the progressive downtown area. He carried a stack of transportation logs for delivery to the Eternal Resource Service.

"Here it is. E.R.S., nineteenth floor, suite B. Now why couldn't Darius have taken care of this before he left?" Gideon thought. "God only knows why he felt the need to enroll in a week long course on database management. These logs are damn heavy, but at least I'll get them in before the 5:00 deadline." Gideon punched the button for the elevator and the door opened. The sound of running feet and heavy breathing sounded in the lobby and Hiram rushed to the elevator.

"Wait, hold the door."

Gideon stuck a hand in the door and Hiram stepped inside, clutching a sealed envelope. He punched button fifteen. "Sir Gideon, is that you? I didn't know you moonlighted as a pack animal. Where's Darius?"

"Well, Hiram. Long time, no see. Not since Robert Smith died. Please don't tell me you've been given another assignment already," Gideon cringed. "I recommended some remedial courses in the Oversight Committee hearing."

"No, actually I've been doing a little writing of my own. Not as scholarly as yours, of course. But, let's say, you've been a real inspiration to me."

"I'm an inspiration to everyone, but I didn't take you for the writing type. Not enough self-discipline." Gideon watched the control panel light up number ten.

"Well, I guess I just needed to find a topic that interests me. Say, do you want to get a drink? There's this great little penthouse cafe at the top of the building. The Cloudburst. Just opened. Brand new. Got great reviews in the Journal of Refreshment. I just need to drop off this envelope on and I'll meet you up there. What do you say?" The control panel lit number fifteen and the door opened.

"Sure, why not. It might be a small compensation for having to lug these logs all the way here." Gideon waved and the door closed.

Suite B on the nineteenth floor was spacious and elegantly decorated with the paintings of the Renaissance masters. A small receptionist hid behind two plants on her desk.

"Ahem...where do these logs get delivered for audit? My assistant usually brings them."

The receptionist looked up. "Are...are you Sir Gideon? I've seen you on all the talk shows. You're even more awesome in person." The receptionist stood up took the logs from Gideon. "I'll put them right over here and make sure they get filed, sir."

"That would be helpful. Carry on." He turned back toward the elevator.

Gideon and Hiram were seated close to a window in the Cloudburst Café.

"You can't beat the view, that's for sure," Hiram surveyed the scene from his chair.

Gideon sat at the opposite side of the table already sipping on a fresh squeezed cirrus drink. Marble-sized balls of the purest hail tinkled against the crystal chalice. "Yes, well, I suppose it is exciting for you to experience this altitude, but I've clocked over 35,000 hours of upper atmosphere flight. Now that's where the view is."

"Whatever..." Hiram mumbled. "I mean what's the weather. What's the weather like, uhm, in the upper atmosphere?" Hiram sipped his Thunderstorm Smoothie.

"Humid," Gideon said dryly. "So enough with the weather talk. What kind of writing have you been doing?"

"Oh, mostly stuff about my experiences, the angels I've met, things I've seen. Not that I've had many experiences, met many angels, or seen anything very interesting. But it keeps me off the streets and out of the pool halls. How's it going with Corey? How's he getting along without his dad? You know, I feel really bad about Robert's death, but I'm not sure I could have done anything differently. Maybe I'm not cut out for guardianship."

"Not everyone is," Gideon said sympathetically. "But don't be too hard on yourself. It's not easy getting back into the game after your stint in the Nether Reaches. Corey's growing up fast. He celebrated his fifteenth birthday last month. He's mostly made the right choices, at least, whenever I was nearby. Except for that one time at computer camp. Corey got lost on his way back from a hike and ended up in the woods at night. Wouldn't you know it, he didn't have his flashlight. So I had to lend him a luminary ball so he could get back to his cabin. Can't have him falling off a cliff or something," Gideon laughed.

"Well, that was protective of you. But weren't you worried about lending out your luminary? He could have extinguished it."

"Nah, Corey's got a pure soul. Anyway, all's well that ends well. Speaking of endings, I'd better get back to the office. I am swamped in fan email since my appearance on the Orpheus Show. See you around, maybe." Gideon stood up and headed toward the door of the café.

Chapter Ten

Gideon strolled into the recording studio with plenty of time to spare. The documentary titled Human Death would not begin shooting until 3:00 p.m. Celestial Standard Time, so he had thirty minutes to look over his notes. The camera crew set up equipment and the light technician experimented with the latest in radiance compression technology. Gideon flipped open his laptop, scrolled down the script he had written for his talk, and then clicked an icon on the screen. He glanced quickly at the image of Corey chewing on his pencil as he contemplated a physics problem.

"Darius," Gideon called switching back to his text. Darius appeared wearing blue jeans and a tie-dyed shirt.

"I need a copy of my 1245 study on grief and that essay I did for the Psychological Research Department. I think it was called "Three Easy Steps to Death" and…what in Heaven are you wearing?" Gideon finally looked up.

"Oh, sorry, sir. It's my day off, but I'm sure you remembered that. Some of the other assistants and I were just on our way to Cumulus Cliff for some bungee jumping."

"You know, sometimes I think we need to bring back the good old days of the Demon Wars just to give you youngsters something to do. Now be sure to get my information *before* you throw yourself off a cloud." Gideon closed up his laptop as Darius disappeared.

"Sir Gideon, we're almost ready for you." A camera technician had just finished adjusting the camera angle. Gideon hurried to the filming area. "Three, two, one, action!"

"Greetings, brothers and sisters of Heaven," Gideon began. "I am here to present to you the culmination of my experience, wisdom, and insight into the phenomenon of human death. I am considered the foremost expert on humanity, having undertaken thousands of guardian assignments, and am quite well versed in human philosophical views on death. In addition, I have put in a cumulative total of at least three million years in the divine presence and have a working knowledge of the mind of God. Since we angels do not experience death, inspired insight is the best research tool for studying this phenomenon. Being both inspired and insightful, I have discovered that humans fall into two categories: those who fear death as the end of all existence and those who accept death as a bridge to a better world. Both, however, are limited ways of viewing what could be quite an enjoyable experience. Human beings should learn to experience death as something of a roller coaster ride, maybe a little scary while it is happening, but inevitably temporary. Naturally, if I were human, I would be one of the ones in the front seat with my hands in the air to get the fullest measure of the thrill." Gideon allowed the smallest ripple of laughter to wrinkle his shining composure. "Well, human beings get only one chance to enjoy the ride, but most are blinded by their fear of the unknown and miss all the excitement. Remember to access the complete text of my on-line article on the subject of death."

The camera technician began feeding previously recorded footage of Gideon working in his office, walking along the Most Highway, and practicing both ancient and modern flaming sword patterns.

"I got it, sir." Darius winked into sight, breathing heavily. He waved a golden disk at Gideon.

"You certainly took your time. I wanted to enlighten my audience with one of my quotations from this report." Gideon snatched the disk from Darius. "I wonder if I need to put you on probation. Maybe you had better drag your halo back out of storage, because if you're late again you'll be back on harp duty."

"Oh, no, sir. I'll be the model of assistant reliability. I just thought, well, because it is my day off…that you wouldn't be needing me, and…"

"Go! I've got work to do," Gideon slid the disk into his laptop.

"Yes, sir, Sir Gideon," Darius saluted. "But, sir, just one more thing…"

"What?" Gideon barked, shimmering around the edges.

"You're standing on my bungee cord, sir."

"We got a card from Rindy today, Mom. It's postmarked in Las Vegas, but no return address." Corey gestured toward the mail stacked on the kitchen table where he was working on algebra homework.

Emma took off her high heels, sat down, and read the postcard. "Well, at least she's okay, but it's been a year since she left and your father passed away. I wish she would come home for a visit sometime. Well, I'd better get packed and get some sleep. I've got to fly to Boston tomorrow."

"Again?" Corey asked. "You just went on a business trip two weeks ago."

"I know, darling, but in this new position, I've got to meet new clients, give presentations, and generally make the company look good. You'll be fine, though. The fridge is already stocked with your favorite frozen dinners. Fifteen is plenty old enough to 'house sit' for a week."

"Sure, Mom. Whatever." Corey attacked another problem.

"Honey, if you weren't such a good, sensible boy, I wouldn't feel like I could leave you. But I'm not worried. You are very responsible and always make the right decisions. Now, I'm going to bed. Try not to stay up too late." She kissed him on the cheek. "What are these bruises on your arm?"

"Oh, we're playing flag football in P.E. and I got tackled," Corey answered.

"Well, try to be more careful. You know you tend to bruise easily. Good night, sweetheart."

"Another 100 percent for Corey. Well, done! Class, Corey has made straight As in algebra for the last three nine-week sessions. You all will have to work pretty hard to catch up with him now." Mr. Dell handed out papers to the rest of the students in the class, most of which took their papers and stuffed them in their desks. "Continue with the homework on exponential notation and be ready for a quiz tomorrow."

After Algebra, Corey and Trent walked down the hall to their lockers. "How can you always make such good grades?" Trent asked. "I'm clinging to a C for dear life."

"I ought to make an F next time just for kicks, but it might give Mr. Dell a heart attack. But it would be worth it to see him raving like a lunatic." Corey dumped his books in his locker and picked up the next set.

"Yeah, he might start foaming at the mouth or something. Oh, and speaking of raving lunatics, how's it going with Operation Conquest?"

"Well, we've had three dates so far and I think she's starting to fall for me."

"You did kiss her, didn't you? Remember, that was on the agenda for the second date?" Trent and Corey hurried back up the hall to history class.

"Not exactly. But at the dance last week I sort of brushed my lips on her cheek."

"That's all?" Trent stopped. "You've got to move faster than that, church boy, or Adair will think you aren't interested."

"I've got it under control, Trent. She's coming to my house this evening after we get a bite at the Patio Café. We're going to watch a movie, and…" he winked. "Mom's away on a trip all week."

"You little devil. Just don't back out at the last moment. And speaking as your official romance advisor, do not have another one of your typical nosebleeds like when you tried out for the swim team. Very uncool, and too gross for a sympathy ploy. Seize the moment. For where your pleasure is, there your heart will be also." Trent waved as he headed to the gym and Corey continued to his last class of the day.

Chapter Eleven

Corey finished adjusting the pillows on the couch for the tenth time when the doorbell rang. He opened it hoping his hair hadn't started sticking up. Adair wore hot pink shorts and a black tank top and her shiny cinnamon hair fell in waves to her shoulders.

"Hmm, interesting." Adair stepped inside and walked into the living room. "I've never been in a duplex before. Are you sure you have the place to yourself?"

"I promise, Adair. My mom is out of town. I rented two great movies, and we can make some popcorn and, look here's a liter of root beer." Corey scanned the inside of the refrigerator.

"Corey, we're not in junior high anymore and actually, I've got a better idea." Adair slid close to Corey and he could smell her shampoo. "I don't suppose you've ever smoked pot." She drew out two carefully rolled cigarettes from her purse.

"Is that marijuana? Where did you get those?" Corey tensed as Adair pressed up against him.

"You did promise that we'd have a good time. Well, I'm just helping you out. You going to get a match?"

"Adair, I…well…can't we just watch a movie or something?"

"Look, all my friends have been telling me to forget about you. That you are too much of a goody, goody nerd, but I stuck up for you. Now shut up and light up, or it's over between us." Adair handed a cigarette to Corey.

Corey stared at the rolled paper and commanded his hesitant hand to take it from Adair. "Okay, okay, I'm cool. Matches are in the kitchen." He walked into the kitchen and began digging around in a drawer. Following him, Adair laid the cigarettes on the counter and began rubbing her hands on his back.

"Well? Some time this century would be nice," Adair whispered in his ear.

Corey dropped the matches on the counter and froze in exquisite discomfort. His heart was racing and his body on fire.

Adair picked up the box of matches, lit one of the joints, and sucked it long and slowly between her shiny pink lips. "Come on, join me." She struck another match and held it toward Corey. He stared deeply into the flame. A flaming sword rose and fell, and with each stroke a line of hideous demons screamed and ran. The evil hordes shielded their eyes against the brilliant light.

"Damn, you idiot. Are you going to light up, or what?" Adair dropped the lighted match on the counter top and rubbed her finger.

"I can't do this. I'm sorry, Adair. I really want to, but I…I don't know."

"I don't need a boyfriend that's either too scared or too righteous to experiment with new things. All the kids are smoking it these days. Why don't you wake up and join the twenty-first century?" She grabbed the joint from Corey, picked up her backpack, and stormed out the door.

Corey flung himself on the couch, grabbed the pillows that he had so carefully arranged, and threw them on the floor.

"Oh, crap! I am so stupid. It was just a stupid cigarette. It's all your fault, Gideon. You're ruining my love life."

"Ah, yes, love. The topic of one of my graduate research projects." Gideon appeared instantaneously. His silver-white wings were still extended and quivered in an unseen breeze. He had changed his usual business suit for a white flight suit and goggles. He sat down in an armchair and flattened his wings into a comfortable position. He looked up expectantly. "You rang?"

"Not exactly. I just blew it with Adair. Now she thinks I'm a loser. And it's all because of you. All those stories about the Great Demon Wars and flaming swords leaping to vanquish evil by the power of the light. You've got my mind so filled up with righteous heroism that I can't even act like a normal kid anymore."

"Then I take it the date was a … what do you call it? A flop?" Gideon said.

"Flop. Disaster. Apocalypse. You could say that. I don't want to hear any more war stories, okay? It's messing with my mind. I just want to be a regular kid who jumps into things without thinking and isn't so bogged down with morality. Why can't I just be normal?"

"If you truly wish it," Gideon said sadly, "I could probably appeal to a Higher Authority and get a memory wipe for you. All of our history together would be just, well, history." Gideon said with forced nonchalance. "Of course, I'll have to cancel my order to have my seven-volume <u>Demon Chronicles</u> translated from Latin for you. No problem. The golden inscription plate can be recycled for something else, a doorknob perhaps. And I was kind of looking forward to teaching you my newest disarm technique. But never mind. No more sword practice. No more conversations. No more accounts of how I've spent my existence in service to the light. My lips are sealed, chapter closed, end of…"

"Wait…" Corey interrupted and sighed. "I didn't mean it like that. I'm sorry. I've practically lived on your stories all my life, and…I guess even Adair isn't as important as your friendship."

Gideon looked up eagerly. "Then you do want me to tell you what I did at the War of the Tower? Those Babylonians were so lucky I was there."

Corey laughed. "Gideon, you're the best guardian angel anyone could hope for. Forget Adair. Someday, I'll find someone better. But, just out of curiosity, why do you still have your wings on? I thought you took them off after flight training?"

"Wings? What wings?" Gideon turned around. "Oh no! I just left twenty five novice flyers loose in United States air space!" Gideon disappeared and Corey heard the echo of his voice. "Disregard any rumors about UFOs that might be reported on tonight's news." Corey was alone again.

"Come on, Trent. It's only a volleyball game." Corey walked the crowded school hallway chewing on a straw he had taken from the cafeteria.

"Yeah, I know how you people operate. First, it's just a volleyball game, then it's a retreat, and then it's sitting in a church service trying to act pious while being bombarded with religious advice that has nothing to do with me. I've been a prisoner in my dad's congregation all my life. 'Great the hate and hollow the way that leads to infernal life.' Count me out," Trent said adamantly.

"Okay, the youth group will just have to win without you," Corey said. "But I don't see why you are so anti-religion. Don't you believe in God just a little bit?"

"Have you seen him?" Trent stopped and Corey turned to face him.

"Well, no, but I know someone who has," Corey offered.

"Oh yeah? Who?"

"I'm not supposed to say," Corey pretended interest in the student council campaign posters on the wall.

"Why do you people always have to be so cryptic? So mysterious? 'I can't say. It's a secret.' Well, I'm not waiting around for 'enlightenment.' The 'afterlife' is too long to wait for a reward. I expect to get mine in this lifetime, compliments of the Deathstalkers. Raven says only the weak-minded still believe all that divinity crap. The real master is our own will. If we want it, we'll get it." Trent silently shuffled some papers in his binder as a group of freshmen girls passed in the hallway. "I've made my choice. I'm getting initiated this weekend and you would be a fool not to join me."

"Initiated? Trent, it's wrong. Gid...I mean my friend says that the promises of evil are an illusion. Raven is leading all of you down a road that dead ends in an eternity of despair. Just don't do it." Corey pleaded.

"You pathetic loser. You don't see, do you? You just can't keep up with the times. God is dead." Trent stalked off toward his fifth hour class as the tardy bell rang. Corey stuck his flattened straw back in his mouth and dragged himself to the chemistry lab.

"Sir, let me do it." Darius took the ends of the golden cord from Gideon's fumbling hands. He knotted it perfectly around the white robes at Gideon's waist and stood back. "There, the golden cord to symbolize service and the knot for eternity. You are now ready to assist at Judgment Court. Good luck, sir." Darius saluted.

Gideon walked nervously up the three small hills toward the vortex of light where Judgment Court had taken place from the beginning of time. The crystalline gates were flung open and angels in their most radiant garb were hurrying in to take their places. The harp orchestra had already set up on a series of clouds directly above the choir. Gideon made his way to the Book of Records at the foot of the marble dais as he had done only twice before when called to court duty. The name on the cover of the great book was Zebediah Quincy.

"Well," Gideon thought flipping the pages. "Judging from the out-of-date name and the thickness of the book, this one has been waiting for judgment for quite some time. This should be interesting." He scanned the pages, oblivious of the bustle of activity around him. The thrones were set up at the top of the dais and a carpet unrolled the length of the stairs, beyond the supplicant's platform, and all the way to the entrance gates.

Trumpets announced the arrival of the Judge, and the throne glowed in radiance as bright as the explosive brilliance at creation's dawn. The angels lining the court shielded their eyes and knelt to honor the divine presence. Gideon lifted the cover of the book to shadow the page he was reading. Zebediah had apparently been a rather reckless young man, especially in his journeys to the sheikdoms of the Middle East. In his best lecture voice, Gideon began to read the life story of Zebediah Quincy as the supplicant entered and knelt for judgment. A long second of eternity passed and Gideon closed the book. As he stepped back toward the witness area, he glimpsed Zebediah sobbing into his hands and a cloud of light enveloping his figure. The harps played the recessional and the choir began a difficult four-part harmony as the angelic assembly began to withdraw. Gideon felt a fleeting surprise at his lingering fascination with the man's life. Beyond the reading of the records, proceedings of Judgment Court were seldom made public unless the tabloid editors deemed the outcome interesting enough to sensationalize in print. Curiosity as to the man's fate burned in his mind. Grace or condemnation?

"I couldn't judge," he admitted to himself.

"Well, that was a juicy one." A voice boomed in his ear.

"Nathan, I didn't see you at court."

"I was called to the trumpet squad this time. It's been a while since you read records, hasn't it? You seemed a little preoccupied." Nathan accompanied Gideon through the crystal archway.

"Have you ever wondered what happens to the supplicants during the time they are enveloped in divine light, Nathan? I mean, what's it like? We never witness anything after the official reading from the Book of Life."

"Well, with a record like that one, I'll bet it wasn't too comfortable. I'd put fifty on fire and another fifty on brimstone for Zebediah's ultimate fate." Nathan laughed. "Come on, let's talk business over dinner at the Borealis Light Bar. My treat."

Chapter Twelve

The two angels entered the Borealis just as a large crowd of junior Gravity Techs was leaving. Gideon picked up a copy of the *Celestial Inquirer* on the way in. They negotiated their way among the noisy tables toward a booth in the back.

"Well, this is turning into quite the day for socializing. Excuse me a minute, Nathan. I believe that's Arelia over there." Gideon headed to a table where a single angel sat bent over a book and made notes in the margins.

"I thought it was you." Gideon said amicably. "How is your case going these days?"

"Oh, Sir Gideon. It's been a while. We just don't bump into each other anymore since Rindy moved out," Arelia answered. "She's alive and well these days, but doesn't seem to want anyone, especially her family, to know where she is."

"Well, that's her choice. She's not an easy case for your first post-graduate assignment, is she?"

"No, sir. But I'm doing this one exactly by the book, your book." She closed and thumped the cover of her copy of How to Guard, volume III. "And I took some extra classes on human dreaming. I believe I'm making progress with her."

"Good work. Be sure she comes to visit her mother and Corey as soon as possible, and let me know if you have any questions about volume III. You really should get it on disk, complete with annotations and cross references."

Gideon joined Nathan at his table and the waiter appeared. "I'll have the Preeminent Sunrise with sprinkles, please." Gideon closed the menu and opened his napkin.

"Yes, sir, and your choice of chalice?" The waiter scribbled on a notepad.

"Silver," Gideon answered.

"Make mine the Incandescent Special in crystal." Nathan handed the waiter his menu and gave Gideon a scrutinizing look. "Sprinkles?"

"Why not? Corey always gets candy sprinkles on his ice cream," Gideon said defensively.

Gideon glanced at the front page headline of the tabloid lying on the table and he froze. "Move Over Prometheus: Shining Sentinel Brings Light to Man."

"What the hell.." Gideon scanned the article. "See, this is what I'm talking about. Someone is leaking information." He thrust the paper toward Nathan.

"Hmmm, should I assume that the Shining Sentinel refers to you? Did you do this?" Nathan looked up.

"Of course, it does. It's one of the affectionate nicknames my fans have been using for centuries. And, yes, I let Corey borrow a luminary ball one night to find the trail back to his cabin. But no one could know that.

Corey and I were alone." Gideon folded the paper and frowned at the table.

"Well, maybe you have a secret admirer. That's plausible, isn't it?" Nathan said as Gideon shrugged to concede the point. "So, let's move on to your favorite topic. How is the lad?"

"I haven't checked on him since early this morning. Let me see how he's doing." Gideon took out his pocket PC and turned it on. A holographic image of Corey bent intently over a chemistry lab table filled the air just above the table.

"I see you've upgraded. I didn't even know the pocket model was available yet. You must have some connections on the Technology Committee," Nathan said and cleared a space on the table for the waiter to place the two chalices. The Preeminent Sunrise bubbled a gentle illumination as the waiter sprinkled a pinch of silvery glitter on the top. The Incandescent Special shone golden with a hint of rainbow aura.

"It's just a prototype, but yes, the Tech Directory owed me a favor. This holographic model is just a creative adaptation of standard halo technology." Gideon watched the holographic image of Corey. "No, not that one, Corey. That one is acid. You can't add an acid to that mixture. Get the other beaker." Gideon held his breath as Corey considered which substance he needed to add to his test tube to complete the reaction and finish his report.

"He can't hear you, by the way." Nathan took a long sip from his chalice.

"Quiet, will you?" Gideon said and turned back to Corey. "The other one, the other one, come on! Yes, that's right!" Gideon sat back and shook his head. "That was a close one. Everyone knows that reaction would have been explosive."

Nathan pushed Gideon's chalice toward him. "Actually I don't think the chemicals were available in sufficient quantity to blow up the high school chemistry lab. Correct me if I'm wrong, but isn't one of the purposes of human life to make mistakes and learn from them?"

"Well, of course," Gideon said irritably. "Human choice and free will are sacred, but this was different. Corey was just making a dangerous mistake. It's not the same thing. Oh, and speaking of human beings, how is yours? Do you know what Trent is doing right now? Are you keeping him under surveillance?"

"Of course. At precisely this moment he is, let me think…" Nathan took another sip and settled into an expression of intense concentration. "He is…making his own choices and…ah, yes…living his own life."

"You wouldn't be implying that I am not letting Corey live his own life, would you?" Gideon stirred his Sunrise and scooped some sprinkles from the top. "Have you forgotten that I am considered the leading authority on principles of guardianship?"

"Oh, I've read your articles in the *Guardian Gazette*, although you haven't published anything recently. And your How to Guard series has been the basis of the training curriculum for centuries. Yes, I'm quite aware of your credentials, Sir Gideon. I'm just curious to know when was the last time you read your own guidelines. I remember a young graduate assistant who taught me long ago that just as we are limited in the area of free will, we are also limited by the extent to which we can influence human action, choice, and will. 'Guide, Don't Give' was your standard."

"It's not like that," Gideon bristled. "You just don't know Corey. If you did, if you could talk to him and learn from him, you would understand. The guidelines and standards are meant to apply to the typical angel-human association, not to special cases like mine, or to a guardian of my rank and skill. And you would do well to monitor your charge's activities more closely." Gideon drained his chalice. "Young Trent needs guidance. Are you aware of his interest in becoming a Deathstalker initiate? Why do I know more about your charge than you do? I wonder if the Eternal Affairs Committee shouldn't take a look at your guardianship logs."

Nathan slammed his empty chalice down heavily on the tabletop. "EA would find everything in perfect order, Sir Gideon. Whatever Trent has done or will do, it is truly his own choice. I have guided; he has chosen. I have exercised my duty; he has exercised his free will. This is the official guardian policy, and you know it!"

"Certainly it is, and you go right on following it," Gideon said getting up and placing his pocket PC in his coat pocket. "And someday when, like me, you are promoted to Chairman of the Guardian Division, you may even be enlightened enough to tell the difference between the spirit and the letter of the law." Gideon stood up to leave.

"Before you go," Nathan said licking the last drops from his spoon. "Let me refresh your memory about the Great Casting Out and what happened to angels who were blinded by their own pride. Poor old Lucifer. And he was such fun at parties."

Gideon turned sharply and left the Borealis Light Bar. Several pairs of angel eyes squinted at the intensity of his aura.

Chapter Thirteen

"Bad day at the office?" Corey looked up from his algebra book.

Gideon sat opposite Corey at the kitchen table staring at the first two paragraphs of his article. "Bad day? Why do you say that?" Gideon tried to look cheerful.

"Well, you've been doing more staring than typing for the last half hour, for one thing. I thought you had to get that article written for your *Daily Divine* column by tomorrow."

"I guess I'm just distracted. The subject of this week is Justice, and I keep thinking about yesterday's Judgment Court. I'm not really sure what slant to take in this article. Besides that, I had a little disagreement with Nathan, you know, Trent's guardian. You don't think I influence you too much, do you?"

"Of course not. Remember you said I should give up trying to get Adair to notice me and I didn't listen. Well, you were right as always. And about the article, didn't you always say that people don't really want justice because perfect justice would mean perfect payment for doing wrong? People ask for justice only for their enemies, but what they want for themselves and their friends and family is mercy. You called it the 'backdoor of justice.'"

"Right. That'll be the focus of the article. Thanks, Cor. By the way what's going on with Trent these days?"

Corey sighed. "It's not looking too good. I never could convince him to come to church with me, or even join the youth group volleyball team. He told me last week that he would be joining Raven's group, the Deathstalkers. There is going to be an initiation ritual. They seem to think they can gain some kind of power that makes them able to escape death. It's pretty crazy."

"Well, be sure you stay far away from them." Gideon shook his head. "Misguided fools."

"You know, Gideon. Don't get mad or anything, but I think I understand a little about why kids would want to join a group like that. Parents, school, the law, and society all control their lives, and they feel like they have no power over anything. I guess they feel like evil power is better than no power at all."

"You might be right, but what's the appeal of power anyway? Human beings have been given free will, and that is by far the greatest power available to them," Gideon said.

"Yeah, but it doesn't really feel all that special. I know you wish you and the other angels had it, but kids want cool powers that they can see, like flying, or being invisible, or instantaneous transportation, or fighting with a flaming sword, or influencing people to get what they want, or being immortal. But every time I try to talk to Trent he doesn't listen. He's going to make a really big mistake, and I have to sit back and watch. I just feel helpless."

"I know the feeling," Gideon said absently.

"You do? I can't imagine the great Sir Gideon ever feeling helpless." Corey shook his head. "What happened?"

"I don't usually like to talk about it, but there was an incident a couple thousand years ago. We call it the dark times. It started with a rumor that our Lord was leaving the protection of Heaven on a mission to Earth. I was elected to head what is now known, in the book a <u>Brief History of Heaven</u>, as the Great Delegation. As a delegation of some of the most enlightened minds in Paradise, we took it upon ourselves to try to convince God of the foolhardiness of this venture. He would be beyond the influence of angelic powers and trapped in a human body, of all things. But even our most carefully developed logic backed up by hundreds of angel-hours of research seemed to fall on deaf ears. He went anyway, and all of Heaven stopped breathing." Gideon's golden aura began to waver.

"Are you talking about the incarnation?"

"Incarnation, incarceration, call it what you will. It was the most agonizing and traumatic time of my existence. I was reduced to a helpless, crying baby, powerless to do anything but watch. In fact some of us had to be physically restrained to keep from seizing our swords and marching on Earth."

"It all worked out okay, though, right?"

"Yes, after the darkness, Heaven was bathed in a brightness more resplendent than ever before. And it hasn't dimmed by even a light wave in all these years. But the memory of those helpless times hasn't dimmed either. So, believe me, I know how you feel."

"Well, you tried, right? I've tried my best with Trent. Maybe we can't save the whole world. So, snap out of it Gideon. Your aura's looking really shabby. Tell me a story about the War. That'll get you out of your slump."

"What about the math? Don't you have a test tomorrow?" Gideon asked.

"Just one story and then I'll get right on to my studying. Please?"

"Well, okay. Have I told you the one about the Tunnelers? No? Well, this was the second major assault after the Rampage at the Front Gate. A group of specially trained tunneler demons dug a hole through time and were planning to appear in the middle of Heaven during our Celebration of the Son. Well, our time monitors got wind of it and my sword division was put in charge of the counter assault. We moved the Courtyard a few minutes into the future and stationed ourselves around the projected tunnel opening. The twelve of us then transformed into cherubim in order to give the appearance of a celebration and to lure the entire legion of tunnelers into the open. When the enemy attacked with their hideous screeching, we instantaneously became a division of seraphim with seven arms and in each arm we wielded a flaming sword."

"Wow, I bet it didn't take long to finish them off," Corey asked excitedly.

"Actually, it took several days, because more legions from the past and future joined the advance group through the time tunnel. It was a glorious battle. The twelve of us with our 84 swords against a sea of evil breaking upon our might like the waves on the shore."

"I wish I could have been there!" Corey waved an imaginary sword through the air in a series of parries and thrusts.

"No, you don't! Fighting legions of evil is not a place for human beings. Even some of my troops found it difficult to resist the insidious lure of evil. And we were even protected by our inability to make a wrong choice. Faced with that compulsion, you and every other human being would have succumbed miserably."

"You certainly don't have much confidence in humanity, Gideon. Not to mention me," Corey joked. "I've got pretty good resistance. I wouldn't have joined up with the enemy if I were there. Duh, I know what evil is."

"Corey," Gideon said gently. "As a human being you have the gift of discernment between good and evil. But, my experience guarding humans has shown me that it is not always easy to choose. You have never seen true evil and in its face even you might forget your gift of choice."

"You know, Gid. You are way too serious. I've already chosen good. Evil isn't even an issue, except for this algebra problem. It's starting to corrupt my soul. Could you give me a hint?"

"Not a chance!" Gideon turned back to his laptop and started typing.

"I knew you'd say that," Corey sulked and began flipping back in the chapter. "Oh, by the way, tomorrow I've got a doctor's appointment so I'll be home late. Mom's taking me."

"Doctor? Are you sick?" Gideon stopped typing.

"Just a pain that has been bothering me. And Mom is all paranoid about my nosebleeds and getting tired all the time. I'm sure it's nothing to worry about. But you know my mom. She thinks there is a medicine for everything. At least I get to miss my last two classes."

"Maybe I should run a scan or something. I can borrow a blood scanner or an x-ray device from my friend in the Bio-spiritual Research Department. You should have told me sooner."

"Gideon, you're my guardian, not my doctor," Corey laughed. "Haven't you ever heard of growing pains? It's probably nothing. Now, if I don't figure out these twenty equations, you're never going to write your article for the column."

Chapter Fourteen

"Leukemia? Are you sure that's what the doctor said?" Gideon walked Corey to school the next day.

"Well, I was in the other room when he was talking to my mom, but I'm pretty sure that's what he called it. Look at my arm. "It's all bruised from those blood samples." Corey held out his forearm. "What's wrong with you? You look whiter than a ghost," he laughed.

"I think maybe you misheard the doctor. Yes, that must be it. I'll talk to you later. I have to check something out." Gideon disappeared in a blink. Corey shrugged and trudged on to school. Fifteen minutes after the tardy bell had rung, he arrived, breathing heavily, at the steps of the school.

"Elina, I haven't seen you hanging around here very often," Gideon said to the angel who hovered just above the dining table. Emma Smith sat reading a heavy medical textbook and frantically flipping through pages.

"Sir Gideon, always a pleasure to see you." Elina bobbed her head. "I check in once in a while, but remember, the woman practically lives at the office. She has taken the day off because of the bad news about her son."

"Then he does have leukemia?" Gideon barely breathed.

"Oh, quite definitely, acute lymphocytic leukemia to be exact. It's a rather fast acting form of blood cancer and…what's wrong, sir?" Elina asked.

Gideon landed on the floor just behind Emma and read the text over her shoulder. "Rapidly fatal due to infection or bleeding…platelet transfusion, chemotherapy, bone marrow transplant…" The words of the text fell like stones in his mind and he reeled backward. "It can't be. He's only fifteen. This is not supposed to happen. There's been a mistake." Gideon exploded with the brightness of a small supernova and Elina shielded her eyes.

Darius jumped up, re-shelved the book he was reading, and began to dust furiously when Gideon appeared in the study.

"Darius, get over here! Get the chairman of the Bio-spiritual Research Department on the line, notify Salvation Central, schedule a conference with the archangels, and put the Disaster Crisis Center on alert. Oh, and contact my old friend, Jeremiah, who works as a clerk for the Office of Predestination." Gideon flipped up his laptop and logged on to the Humanity Research Database.

"Yes, sir! May I ask, sir, is there a problem?" Darius fumbled with the phone.

"Of course, there's a problem. Someone has made a major mistake, and I'm going to do something about it."

"The DCC is on the line, sir," Darius announced a few minutes later," and they want to know how many human souls have been affected by the disaster."

"Tell them one," Gideon answered.

"Uh…they said they only deal with disasters with a 1000-soul minimum." Darius shrugged. "I'll call the archangels, sir." He punched a rapid succession of numbers. "It's a recording. 'To everything there is a season, please leave a message.' Would you like me to leave a message?"

"Just give me the phone." He snatched the receiver and dialed. "Jerry, it's Gideon. How are they treating you at the OP…that good, is it? …Listen, I need you to retrieve a file for me…What? All predestination files have been classified…what do you mean you don't have access?" Gideon slammed down the phone and put his head on his desk. A fiery aura lit up behind him like a halo.

"Something has happened to Corey?" Darius tiptoed toward the desk.

"He's dying, Darius." Gideon shook his head. "And I can't do anything about it."

"Hurry up, Gideon, or we'll have to wait in line for tickets." Corey dragged the angel through the crowd. "I'm really glad you agreed to see this movie with me. I'm kind of surprised that you said yes when you hate horror movies. This one's not too bad, though."

"You know I'd do anything for you, don't you, Corey?" He stopped and took the boy's hand.

"Sure, Gid. Now you're not going to get all mushy about how this might be our last movie together, are you?" Corey laughed.

"Of course not! You'll get treatment and make a full recovery."

"That's what I told Mom. After all, not everyone has such a cool guardian angel. I know you'll cure me." Corey continued toward the ticket office.

"Wait, Corey. I meant chemotherapy, radiation, and bone marrow transplant, stuff like that. I have no power to cure you." Gideon looked at the ground.

"Oh, right," Corey scoffed. "I'm supposed to believe that the greatest of Heaven's warriors can't even cure a little human illness? Come on, I know you've got the power. Surely you agree that there is nothing good about being terminally ill. As my guardian you're going to help me fight this evil, right?"

"Corey, I've already sworn to light, to guard, and to guide, and I'll be with you through this whole ordeal. But, your illness isn't evil, and evil didn't make you sick. The victory of good or evil depends on you, on how you let this change you. Let me put it this way. Is fire good or evil?" Gideon stopped walking and faced Corey.

"It's good. It keeps people warm," Corey said.

"But it also burns people. So, again, is fire itself good or evil?"

"I know what you want me to say. That fire is neutral, and what it is used for is either good or evil depending on people's choice. But we're talking about my leukemia, not some nebulous analogy." Corey kicked at a soda can in the parking lot.

"Your illness is neutral, too, but it's your choice as to how to react to it. You can't simply make it disappear, just as you can't make fire non-existent. Corey, it isn't that I don't have the power to cure you. I could snap my fingers and you would be well. But I am forbidden to do it. It would violate every principle of guardianship and rip the very fabric of human freedom. Good versus evil isn't the issue. It's just that eventually humanity manifests all possibilities."

Corey stared at the angel. "Well, that sounds like a bunch of crap to me. Let me get this straight. You can prevent me from dying a horrible death at the age of fifteen, but you just won't? That's a pretty lame excuse. You're just a washed-up failure of a guardian, and you don't even care about me." Corey shouted into the air in front of the theater as the growing crowd watched. "Well, who needs you? From now on you are officially my ex-guardian." Gideon vanished instantly. "And don't call me; I'll call you," Corey shouted as tears filled his eyes.

"Gideon, you're back?" Darius sprang up from the couch.

"Schedule me an extended lecture tour of the Nether Regions. It's been a while since I visited there. Book me for a slot starting tomorrow."

"Yes, sir. But isn't that what you used to call the Celestial Siberia, the Edge of Eternity, the Dregs of Divine Desolation, the…"

"Never mind what I said. It's time for a long vacation. Pack my things while I dig up some lecture notes. Make a reservation for the Happy Harper Hotel. Just email my schedule and make all necessary arrangements." Gideon rummaged through a file while

Darius packed a change of clothes in a suitcase and then reached for the golden laptop.

"No, leave that thing here. I won't be needing it," Gideon snapped.

"But what about Corey, sir?" Darius said.

"Forget Corey. He doesn't need me, and I don't need him. Now give me that suitcase." Gideon took the packed suitcase, grabbed his coat from the hook and opened the door.

Darius stared at his back. "I never thought I'd see the great Sir Gideon, Shining Sentinel, Warrior of Light, Champion of Heaven, Guardian of Humanity, just give up and walk away."

"Shut up!" The door slammed.

Corey walked the long hall from his locker to his first-hour class. Clusters of girls fell silent as he passed and whispered to each other. Students hurrying to classes made brief eye contact and quickly looked away. Corey saw Adair in a group of sophomore girls and purposefully ignored her. Her girlfriends pushed her into Corey's path and she spoke shyly.

"Corey, wait a minute…I…uhm. I just wanted to give you something before you go."

Corey stopped and looked at her suspiciously. She reached up and kissed him quickly on the lips. "After all, you haven't lived until you've been kissed." She disappeared into her group of giggling girls. Corey adjusted the baseball cap that he had been given special permission to wear inside the building. The last two weeks of chemotherapy had reduced his heap of brown hair to a straggle bordering on baldness.

"You can keep your pity!" he shouted at the girls.

"Well, if it isn't the church boy. And looking more monkish by the day." Trent stepped out from behind a locker door. He wore a black sleeveless shirt that revealed a tattoo on his upper arm, a skull with a dagger in its mouth.

"What do you want? The bell's about to ring." Corey tried to push past.

"I heard that death's got an eye on you, and don't you deny it. 'Oh death, here is thy sting.' You know that chemo-crap isn't going to save you. Too bad you're just too chicken to live. The Deathstalkers can offer immortality for a very reasonable price. Who do you think can save you? Doctors? Mommy? That little imaginary angel you used to talk to?"

Corey froze and turned to face Trent.

"Oh, I've heard you deep in conversation with your little fairy-friend. But I wonder where he is now? He doesn't seem to be anywhere around here." Trent looked Corey over. "No, not sitting on the shoulder. No, not in the book bag." He came closer. "Not even in the pocket. I guess that's friendship for you. Leave them when the going gets tough."

"I don't know what you're talking about," Corey said quietly.

"The truth hurts, doesn't it?" Trent said in mock sympathy. "I asked you once before, and I'll ask one last time. Join the Deathstalkers and live forever, or die in agony as disease gnaws you from within. We are meeting at midnight a week from Friday at Ben's Clearing in the north woods." Trent drifted off just as the first-hour bell rang. "You can only depend on yourself."

Chapter Fifteen

"Corey, darling," Emma called. "Are you getting dressed?" Hearing no answer she gave her hair one last spray and then knocked on her son's door. "Corey? You're not even out of bed. Are you feeling worse today?"

"Just tired," Corey mumbled from under his blankets. "Don't want to get up today."

"But honey, you have a history test today, don't you? Come on, let me make you some toaster waffles before I drive you to school." Her voice sounded overly sweet, as she tried too hard to sound cheerful and optimistic.

"Don't want to eat. I hate food. Let me sleep." Corey pulled his covers up tighter and his mother sat down on the bed and patted the part of the lump that might have been his back.

"Okay, sweetie. Maybe you can skip school today. I'll call in your excuse, but you need to be up by 3:30 when Miss Kathy comes to take you to your treatment. You know she has other patient visits scheduled and insists on being on time for appointments."

"Yeah, I know. I sure don't want to be late for my daily dose of chemicals. I already feel like a toxic waste dump."

"Now, the doctor feels that chemotherapy is the best treatment for you, and it's only been three weeks. I bet you'll be feeling better before too much longer. Get a bowl of cereal when you feel like eating, and remember, the doctor said small frequent meals. Now, I've got a meeting this morning at 9:00, but I'll call you if I get a break." She bent over and kissed Corey's forehead and left the room.

"Uh…Sir Gideon? We are ready for your book signing in the Gold Room, and the line is already forming." The concierge of the Happy Harper Hotel spoke from the doorway. Gideon, sitting at a table on the patio, gathered up the rows of playing cards and ended his game of Solitaire. He rose slowly and followed the other angel into the hotel. "By the way, sir, some of the staff are planning an afternoon recreational flight. The jet stream has made its yearly change in course and makes for some interesting wind currents. If you'd like to join us…"

"I'm sure you and your staff will enjoy your little diversion, but an official of my status and caliber is much too busy to devote time to recreation. In addition to being the Chairangel of the Committee on Guardian Affairs, I am a contracted columnist for several publications, I am a professor of humanology at the University of Heaven at Paradise, I am the senior instructor at the School of Swordsmanship, not to mention an Alpha Class aviator with more experience in flight than your entire staff combined. Now if you will excuse me, I have a roomful of fans to meet." Gideon adjusted his halo to full light spectrum and arranged the gold handkerchief in his coat pocket before entering the Gold Room. With an air of unhurried importance he waved to the crowd of waiting fans and took a chair at the signing table.

"I just love your books, sir." An angel in a long robe, at least two centuries out of style, held a worn copy of <u>The Science of Worship</u>. "We don't get much of the new stuff out here, but your books have been around for centuries. I just never thought I'd actually be meeting you and having you sign my book. I'm just ever so thrilled."

"Yes, of course you are. And just what line of work are you in?" Gideon signed the title page with a flourish.

"I'm on the weather squad right now, but I've got big plans to move on up the ladder to biosphere and ecosystem and maybe even work on the Gaia Project someday."

"How very interesting," Gideon yawned. "Next?"

A very young angel timidly approached the signing table and deposited a scrap of paper. "Could I have your autograph, sir? You've been my hero ever since I first heard the story of your victory at Rebellion Ridge. I'd give anything to see your sword in action, sir."

"Well, now, youngster. I might have something for you, seeing that you are one of my fans." Gideon signed the paper and then reached into his coat pocket. "Ah yes, here it is."

"Wow, a holographic crystal of the great Sir Gideon brandishing his flaming sword! I'll be the envy of everyone in Humidity Maintenance. Thank you!" He left clutching the autographed paper and the crystal.

"Next," Gideon said.

"How long have you been a nurse, Miss Kathy?" Corey asked. He sat in the front seat as Kathy pulled out of the driveway and onto Oakleaf Avenue.

"Nearly eight years now, and still loving it," she answered.

"You mean you actually like driving patients around to appointments?"

"Oh, that's not all I do. I mostly visit my homebound clients, check their vital signs, administer medications, IV fluids, oxygen. I'll probably be visiting you at home more often in the coming weeks."

"So, you're saying I'll be getting worse?"

"Corey, I didn't mean it like that. But I have taken care of other leukemia patients and I recognize the progression of the illness. Chemotherapy is a treatment, not a cure. Keep your spirits up. Miracles happen every day."

"Yeah, right," Corey mumbled.

"Have you heard from your sister? Rindy, isn't it?"

"Not yet, but Mom has hired a private detective to locate her. She hasn't even heard about my leukemia, but I don't really care if she comes home or not. She's probably trying to get the most out of life while she can. I would."

Kathy drove to the entrance of the hospital.

"Listen. I'll pick you up about 5:00, so when you finish your chemo just wait in the chapel and I'll meet you there."

"Whatever," Corey said and he climbed out of the car.

"You'll be a little nauseated this evening and tomorrow, Corey. I have increased your dose by half. Have you been eating well?" The doctor scanned the lab results as the nurse put away the syringes and vials of medications.

"Not really. I hate food. It makes me feel worse. Do I get to see my lab results or is it classified?" Corey rolled down his sleeve.

"Well, your white blood count and platelets are down. Let's see. Uric acid, potassium, and phosphate levels elevated. I think it is time to start IV fluids and perhaps think about a platelet transfusion. You really need to eat small, frequent meals to help with the nausea." The doctor wrote new medication orders and switched to a more powerful broad-spectrum antibiotic.

"Is this chemo stuff going to work, Dr. Robinson? Or are you just pumping me full of chemicals so that when I die I'll already be partially embalmed?"

Dr. Robinson took off his glasses and looked up at Corey, still sitting on the examination table. "Son, you're old enough to know the truth. The form of leukemia that you have, acute lymphocytic, is known to be rapidly fatal due to infection or bleeding. You have said that the headaches, nosebleeds, abdominal pain, weakness, and bruising have become more pronounced lately. This shows a rapid progression of the illness. We may consider a bone marrow transplant, but it's not a guarantee."

"So, what exactly are my chances of seeing my sixteenth birthday?" Corey asked.

"Truthfully, if the disease progresses along the rate we have seen these last three weeks, you may have only a matter of months left to live. I know this is hard to hear at your age, and there may yet be a remission which will increase your time, but there is still no cure for this type of leukemia. Because of the increased dosage this time, I'll need to see you back in three days. Is Kathy taking you home?"

"Yeah." Corey slid off the examination table. "I'm supposed to meet her downstairs. Thanks, Doc."

"Hang in there, son. Keep praying."

Corey took the elevator down the three floors to the lobby and looked for the hospital chapel. He paused at the chapel door and looked in. Several people were inside, some sitting with bowed heads and some kneeling. A statue of Christ stood expressionless in a corner, and a small white altar added only a dull presence to the stagnant air. Corey went inside and took a seat near the door. The familiar nausea that followed his treatments began, and he felt sick. He tried to pray, to find those neglected pathways that he used to walk as a child. They were gone, and he found no presence, either divine or angelic, to acknowledge his existence, much less his pain.

"To hell with this," Corey said loudly and stood up. Bowed heads turned toward him and he fled the chapel.

"You're awfully quiet, Corey," Kathy said, finally breaking the silence in the car. "How did the treatment go? How long had you been sitting on the sidewalk?"

"Not long. I feel too nauseated to talk right now."

"You could have waited in the chapel, you know. Sorry I was late. I had to change a catheter for one of my clients," Kathy said.

"No problem. I was busy throwing up in the bathroom anyway," Corey said.

"I know you must feel terrible. The treatment is almost worse than the disease sometimes. But keep praying. I have been working with terminal patients for a long time and I know that prayer really helps them."

"Helps them die more quietly, you mean," he said cynically. "Look, just take me home so I can be sick in peace, will you?"

Kathy drove on in silence and dropped him off at home just as dusk was settling. He let himself into the house and poured himself a bowl of crackers. He sat down and tried to study his history notes. As his mind wandered, his pencil doodled. A small skull with a dagger in its mouth stared back at him from the margins.

Chapter Sixteen

Gideon bumped along the winding road in a two-seat, glassed-in chariot, typical transportation in the nether regions with its high ionization. The lack of reception necessitated alternative transportation, but Gideon missed the use of his instantaneous transporter. The two chariot seats faced each other, but he never sat in the rear-facing seat since moving backward tended to make him nauseous. He typed sporadically at his pocket PC portable keyboard that bounced precariously on his knees. The pair of white unicorns did their best to make sure the wheels met each and every rut as they trotted through the swirling mist. The sub-junior angel who had been assigned as his driver was nodding off to sleep.

"Damn this low-tech crap!" He closed his keyboard in disgust and tried to find any object of interest in the nebulous expanse outside the window. He had left small but enthusiastic audience at the Rise 'N Shine Inn that morning and had been headed North for hours. Three weeks in the outer perimeter had been steadily scraping away at Gideon's usually cheerful confidence. His destination was a detour from the typical lecture circuit since the commander at the Northern Gate had heard that

Heaven's highest ranking sword-master was in the area and had begged a seminar for his troops.

Hours later, and leagues out of his way, Gideon arrived at the Northern Gate camp and disembarked from the chariot. The welcoming party had assembled, a straggly line of angel-soldiers with mismatched armor and rusty swords.

"Welcome, Sir Gideon! We are immensely honored by your presence and can't thank you enough for taking time from your busy schedule to conduct a swordsmanship seminar for us." The commander ushered Gideon into the officers' lounge as the troops quickly dispersed to the practice arena, eager to get a front row seat.

"Let me offer you some refreshment before we begin. I know it's a grueling trip."

"That would be an understatement. But, yes, I could use an Effervescent Fountain with a hint of strawberry if you have it. And I will need to borrow a practice sword for demonstration since I had my own sent on ahead to the Cloud Nine where I will be staying tonight."

"Actually all we have to drink here is pure cloud precipitation, but it's been in full sunlight for hours and is quite refreshing," the commander said humbly.

"Whatever! Just bring it and let's get on with this."

"I have officially modified the Primus Incursus, the most ancient and basic sword technique, to conform to our more modern standards. It includes an inside left parry followed by an immediate lunge at both the alpha and omega points and serves to still the mind and strengthen the soul for more effective resistance against evil incursion." Gideon held the borrowed sword in his right hand in an en garde position and willed it to flame. When nothing happened he concentrated harder and the sword burst into ragged brilliance. "Damn this humidity!"

"When I begin the demonstration I want you to notice the changes from the old pattern. First, the initial stance is thus…the Levitas rather than the Gravitas." Gideon rose in the air until his feet were about two inches above the practice floor. "In the first half of the pattern there is a feint followed by a charge to the opponent's outside from which he begins his strike, and then an attack high, a lateral counter, and a circular disengage."

He launched into a complicated pattern of thrusts, parries, and lunges accompanied by footwork that left his audience in awe. The final technique, perfected by centuries of practice, was a rising cut from the back guard, a 360 degree turn, and a vertical strike downward.

The cheering from the audience snapped Gideon back from his consuming focus and he graciously acknowledged the adoration with a slight bow of his head. For the next two hours, pairs of gate guards practiced the new pattern while Gideon moved among them offering pointers, advice, and a few well-deserved chastising comments.

"No, thrust here; this is your line of attack! Wait, that maneuver is meant to deflect the strike! That counter should be a rising cut from the back guard! You…, correct that stance! Stop, do it over, and this time don't drop the point as you move! Always execute a full cut from the high guard and end in the low guard. This is your high guard and this is your low guard, get it? High guard, low guard. This is hopeless!"

Later that afternoon, Gideon, thoroughly exhausted, climbed back into his chariot to continue with the day's itinerary, a quick trip through Breath Valley and then guest of honor at a dinner with the Perimeter Improvement Steering Committee.

"Oh joy, that should be the highlight of my whole day. At least I get to do another lecture tomorrow. One of my favorite subjects, Evil." Gideon chewed on the end of his stylus as he read the screen of his pocket PC. As the wispy atmosphere floated by, his thoughts drifted to a teenage boy asleep in a lonely house. He jerked his thoughts back. "Damn the reception out here. I can't even get Network." He tapped a few icons on his pocket PC in frustration. "No Net, no news, can't even access my online library. What a bunch of crap! Is anyone even out there?" He settled on a game of Solitaire to occupy his mind and sank wearily into the seat of the chariot. "I'll sell my soul if the Cloud Nine Budget Motel has a spa."

Corey had spent the day in bed tuned in to the distance learning web site for homebound kids where arrangements had been made for him to continue his 10th grade curriculum, English, Algebra II, U.S. History, and Chemistry. He had to drop his electives Art, PE, and Music Appreciation since they were not offered by the online school. At least he'd have enough credits to finish up his sophomore year.

"Not that it matters in anyway whatsoever, since I'll be dead before starting 11th grade. Why the hell am I even doing this?" He threw his notebook on the floor, lay back, and picked absentmindedly at the bowl of pretzels on his nightstand. He sipped slowly on a glass of precipitation. No, just plain old water! It was only four o'clock and his mom wouldn't be home for at least another hour. Feeling nauseous again, he crawled slowly out of bed and lurched into the bathroom. After trying unsuccessfully to throw up, he stumbled back to bed and spotted a toy wooden sword in the corner, a birthday present from another age. Carrying it to bed he remembered the lessons taught to him by one of the best swordsmen in the universe. Parry, thrust, lunge, riposte. Corey went through the motions with the zeal of a zombie. "What's the goddamn point?" He threw the little sword across the room breaking it cleanly in two sections on the opposite wall and buried his face in his pillow. "There is no goddamn point to anything. My life is shit! I might as well join the Deathstalkers. I sure don't have anything to lose."

Chapter Seventeen

Late Friday night, Emma was already asleep when Corey heard his alarm clock go off under his pillow. The digital display showed 1:00 AM. In the darkness Corey got out of bed fully dressed and put on his tennis shoes. He crept to the front door and let himself out under a clear black sky. The full moon made his shadow weak and blurry as he walked along the street. The north woods were only about two miles from Oakleaf Avenue, but he had allotted an hour to walk at his usual slow pace. An occasional motor sounded in the distance, but the road led through a quiet suburban neighborhood and past an isolated section of town near the edge of the woods. He stopped twice to catch his breath and held a tissue to his nose for a few minutes to stop a nosebleed.

The woods loomed up darkly against the black sky, and Corey walked the remaining distance under the heavy limbs of the ancient oak trees of Ben's Clearing. He heard voices ahead and hurried. In the clearing he could see part of a stone wall, crumbling in places and covered with a black cloth. Groups of black-robed figures stood in clusters.

"Well, well, look who decided to show up." Trent appeared from behind a tree. "You must be here to join the ranks of the immortals. Because surely you don't intend to try and win any converts here," Trent laughed and gestured to the gathering crowd, faces hidden within their hoods.

"No, I'm here to join you. The doctor says I don't have much longer to live, and I sure as Hell don't want to die. No one can help me…so I just thought that…well, if what you say is true…then…" Corey swallowed hard.

"Well, you've come to the right place, assuming the master finds you worthy to serve. But, just out of curiosity, what made you change your mind and finally get rid of your childish beliefs? You were always such a little preacher boy."

"What can I say? I was stupid. I thought somebody could save me. But now I know that I can only depend on myself. So, let's get on with it."

"Well, come on, then. We're about ready to start." Trent led him through the crowd. "Raven," he called. "We have another guest at the table tonight."

Raven finished placing an iron goblet on the altar and slowly turned around. Trent presented Corey to the dark-haired man. Raven had grown a thick beard in the years since Corey last saw him. His hollow face shoved his cheekbones up toward his eye sockets and the whites of his eyes gleamed yellow in the moonlight.

"Another initiate to the dark," he hissed looking at Corey with interest.

"And, I might mention, Christian," Trent said with a confident smile.

"An even greater triumph for our Dark Master." Raven's teeth glinted in the moonlight.

"Get him an initiation robe and assign him to the novice group for instruction. I need you to help in the preparations."

They were dismissed with a gesture and Trent led Corey to a group of five young men and women reciting urgent chants in whispered voices. A man with an iron chain around his neck brought a coarse black robe and instructed Corey to remove all clothing and to put on the robe and hood. He threw his clothes and shoes in a heap under a bush and slipped into the heavy robe. The novice hurriedly taught Corey some of the responsorial chants and then ushered his group toward the altar. In a world of dreams and shadows Corey followed the initiates to their places. The robe felt rough against his bare skin and he stepped painfully on exposed sticks and pinecones.

The ceremony began with an invocation to the Lord of Darkness. Behind the altar Raven raised his arms and flung back his head. "Master, I summon you into our presence. Heed the call of your servant, on whom you have bestowed the power to invoke your name. In the name of Satan, I call down the spirit of thunder and lightening." The sky rolled with thunder and a streak of lightening ripped open the sky.

At the name of Satan, Corey felt a cold greasy hand clutching at his heart and he shivered. He looked behind him toward the path he had walked into the clearing but saw only the rapturous gazes of the worshipers. The thunder rolled again overhead at the command of the man at the altar. "You offer us power over death and authority over the elements of nature. You require only our obedience and worship. Be present among your faithful, Lord." Raven lowered his arms, and stillness fell on the clearing. The light breeze Corey had felt moments before ceased. Heaviness descended. "The Master has come."

"Lord of Evil, give us power." The congregation began chanting as Trent held the iron goblet in front of Raven who took a knife from the altar and raised it to his left hand. With one swift stroke he cut his palm and squeezed a thin stream of blood into the waiting vessel. "Let the initiates approach their master and be branded with the mark of servitude."

Corey, along with the other initiates, was guided to the altar and stood in a row as Raven approached with the goblet of blood. The chanting of the other worshipers grew more frenzied. "After receiving the mark of evil, you will kneel as a sign of your submission. Only then will the power of darkness be yours," Raven said as he dipped his thumb into the cup. He traced a line of warm blood with his thumb on the forehead of the first initiate who immediately fell to his knees.

Corey waited with apprehension as Raven made his way down the row. He felt a brooding presence by the altar, watching, waiting. Corey searched the sky and surrounding trees, but the darkness was a thick blanket over the clearing. The cloaked initiate to his left knelt and Raven raised his bloody finger to Corey's forehead.

"What you do this night, you do willingly, Christian." He drew a vertical smudge of blood. "With this sign receive immortal life, but know that our master is ravenous and will gnaw at your spirit as the cancer gnaws at your body."

Corey felt the weight of the mark on his forehead dragging him to the ground and he knelt and bowed his head. He heard a shrill cry of triumph from the darkness that surrounded the unholy altar. In Corey's mind a dim image of a figure in immaculate white blurred and faded, replaced by despair as deep as the bottomless pit that reaches into the depths of hell.

The dark ritual continued to encroach upon Corey's dazed mind and he found himself circling the altar with the others, chanting words he did not recognize, and drinking wine, spiked with bitter herbs, from a communal bowl. Time was suspended as Corey found his actions and responses beyond the control of his conscious mind. He did not even notice the progression of the moon across the sky or the slow thinning of the crowd as worshipers drifted away.

As his foggy mind began to clear, he found himself alone for the first time. Corey lurched toward the surrounding trees and stumbled blindly through the undergrowth, gasping for breath in the oppressive darkness. The hem of his robe snagged on a bush, and he felt thorns tearing at the skin on his legs. He cried out as sharp sticks stabbed his bare feet. He clutched the trunk of an oak tree and tried to stop the swaying of the world. Kneeling on the roots, he threw up until he felt he would retch up his entire stomach. Still moaning, he finally lay down and succumbed to unconsciousness in a submission even more compelling that of the Dark One.

"Thank you. You've been a great audience." Gideon waved to the standing crowd tilting his face so as to make the most of the sub-standard lighting in the meeting room. He was speaking to a group of ozone maintenance technicians with a scattering of graduate research students and itinerant harpists touring the outer districts. "I have time for only a few more questions, and in the interest of time, please limit your comments to the topic of my lecture, Evil and the Human Will. Yes, in the front?"

"Sir, you made reference to the use of a word to dispel evil influences. If a word is all that is necessary, why did Heaven fight such a long and tedious battle against the forces of evil back in the Demon Wars?" An angel stood on the back row with wings still dripping from her shift in the upper atmosphere.

"An intelligent question, finally. Actually the power is not in the word itself, but in the will behind the word. As you know, and I have so recently reiterated, angels do not have free will as human beings do. Therefore, we must fight with more conventional means. Whereas human beings have but to state either their acceptance or their rejection of evil, and it comes or goes according to that will."

"Yes?" Gideon pointed to a junior angel in the middle of the audience frantically waving his hand. The angel stood.

"I've just finished my B levels, and was wondering when we get to learn this word which the incarnates use against the enemy forces. I know you said that it is useless without the will behind it, but I've got to know. Is it some ancient Babylonian power word, or one lost even to the writers of the first Bible?"

"I'm surprised you haven't figured it out already, but I can see that the educational system out here is in dire need of restructuring. The word I was referring to has existed in all human languages from the beginning of time. The word is simply "no." A willful and deliberate rejection of evil by even the weakest of human beings is enough to dispel Satan himself. Now, if you will excuse me, I must get to my next scheduled appearance. Books and tapes of this and all of my previous lectures are available as usual and can be ordered from my website on the Heaven Wide Web, hww.sirgideon.god. Fan mail is always welcome. However, keep letters brief and to the point. Thank you."

Gideon gave a final wave and left the podium followed by the sound of enthusiastic applause. Checking his watch, he picked up his hand-held and began scrolling through his itinerary. Thank God the humidity hadn't ruined it. Suddenly, he felt a hand on his shoulder and turned to look.

"Darius? What in Heaven are you doing out here? Did you miss me already?"

"Oh, no, sir. I mean, of course I did, sir. But that's not the reason I came."

Corey woke covered in dew. The pre-dawn sky glowed pink and gray. He stared down at the torn black robe clinging to his body like an oily residue. He looked around for the clearing where he had laid aside his clothes. He was seized with a sudden impulse to tear off the filthy garment and then disrobed enough to shiver in the frosty morning air. Helplessly he pulled the warm robe back around him. Disgust crept over him like a sticky shadow and he remembered the events of the previous night. The evil presence had waited and watched, powerful and compelling. It seemed like another person had accepted the mark on his forehead, knelt in submission, and accepted the rule of evil. The memories were a blur of insanity. He felt his forehead and rubbed a sticky brown substance onto his palm.

"What have I done?" he whispered. The woods were silent. He shook his head. "No!" The wail of anguish wrenched the remaining strength from his desolate spirit. He fell on the ground and sobs wracked his body. "Oh please, help me… Gideon!"

The forest lit up in a white iridescence and the angel appeared in full angelic regalia with wings unfurled, a halo of splendor, and a flaming sword challenging the darkness. Gideon's expression softened as he saw a figure huddled on the roots of a tree. He sheathed his sword, knelt by the wretched boy, and gathered him in a warm embrace. The great and the small held each other until the first rays of dawn filtered through the leaves above.

Chapter Eighteen

"Gideon, I've failed you." Corey buried his face in the angel's robe and wept bitterly. "I am an evil person. You shouldn't even be touching me. I hate myself!" Corey tried to pull away, but Gideon held him closer.

"Child, enough tears. Let's try and salvage what's left of your soul." He patted the boy on the back and stroked the few strands of hair on his scalp. "That's better. Crying is the first step, but tears have done their work now. It's time to stop." He licked his thumb and rubbed the bloody mark off the boy's forehead. "Take off this filthy cloak." Gideon raised Corey to his feet and helped him disrobe. He snapped his fingers and a neatly folded pair of jeans, a blue t-shirt, and a pair of old tennis shoes appeared.

Corey stood up wobbly and dressed. Gideon knelt to tie his shoelaces. "There we go, son. All set." Corey stared at the ground in silence, unable to look into the deep blue eyes of his guardian.

"Come, walk with me." Gideon led the boy to a forest path. The pair walked on in silence as the yellow leaves quivered in an early morning breeze.

After a few minutes, Gideon broke the silence. "Corey, I'm sorry I left. I...I...shouldn't have let my pride get in the way. I should have stayed with you."

"You're forgetting one important detail," Corey said. "I was the one who left you. I was so angry that I blamed you and convinced myself I never wanted to see you again. Looks like I've made a real mess of my life." Corey wiped his nose on his sleeve.

"So, what was it like? What did it really feel like to choose evil?"

"I don't know. It's all just a blur. I think something just came over me and I couldn't think of anything else."

"What kind of something?" Gideon prompted.

"I can't really explain it. What's it like for you never to choose evil? Doesn't something come over you?"

"Not really. Choice is not an issue."

"It must be nice to be so sure of always being good," Corey sulked.

"Well, I think it must be very interesting to have to choose everyday, every hour, every minute. Think of how often you can please God. I feel breathless just thinking about it."

"How would you know? You don't even breathe. Besides you can never, ever disappoint God, like I did. I've been such a fool," Corey said.

"So you have," said Gideon. They walked on in silence.

Corey stopped abruptly. "I can't go on! Gideon, you should leave. I have defiled myself and am not worthy to even be in your presence." He turned away and hid his face in his hands.

"Look. Let's cut the self-pity crap." Gideon turned the boy to face him. "Do you want me to condemn you? Would that make you feel better? Well, too bad. Condemning is not in my job description. You obviously thought that participating in that satanic ritual would give you power, immortality, the ability to fold origami. God only knows what you were thinking. Do you feel better now? Are you powerful? Immortal? No? Okay, so evil took the victory. Now take it back!"

Corey fell to his knees. "I'm sorry. I'm an idiot."

"Do you renounce evil in all its forms?" Gideon asked.

"Yes, I do!"

"If Satan offered you power right now, what would you say?"

"Hell, no!"

"If you were asked to serve and worship evil, what is your answer?"

"No, for God's sake!" Corey cried. "Do you think He can ever forgive me?"

"Rise, son of God, child of the light, beloved of Heaven. You are forgiven."

Corey raised his head and looked at the radiant face of Gideon. "Is that all? Shouldn't I be punished?"

"Oh, you've done that. Now get up and let's move on." Gideon pulled the boy to his feet. "So you stumbled in the path of life. Big deal. Most people do."

"Most people lie or steal. They don't sell their soul to the devil," Corey muttered.

"Did you mumble something?" Gideon asked.

"Gideon, I know you love me no matter what, although I don't know why. You're here, aren't you? But God can never forgive what I have done. Did you see me? I allowed that mark of evil on my forehead. I knelt and worshiped Satan. I drank from his cup. Trent was right.

What I did, I did of my own free will. How can God forgive that?"

Gideon shook his head and sighed. "Seems you're even more of an idiot than I had thought. What do you want, a neon sign flashing 'You are forgiven"? How about a burning bush, or a dove descending from Heaven? Maybe it will take an earthquake or an eclipse to convince you. Maybe a fiery chariot streaking across the sky. Or just maybe you will have to scrounge up enough faith to believe it. God forgives all those who ask for it in sincerity and repentance. And you have just qualified. You are forgiven and the slate is wiped clean. Now, forgive yourself."

Corey looked away. "Even if God forgives me, and I'm not convinced that He has, I can never forgive myself. I knew better."

Gideon sighed and shook his head. "Let's just get you home. We'll talk about it later." He recited his transportation code, touched Corey's head, and the forest path was empty except for a sprinkle of golden glitter that fell softly to the ground.

"Honey, wake up." Emma stood at Corey's bedside. "Are you feeling well enough to study today?"

"What's the point, Mom? You and I both know that I'm dying. It's really irrelevant whether I die before or after taking a test on the presidents of the late 20th century." Corey flung the covers off and sat up in bed. He rubbed his hands through the few remaining hairs on his head.

"Don't say that!" Emma looked horrified. "You are not going to die. We'll do whatever it takes!"

"No!" Corey said abruptly shaking his head. "There are some things I won't do. Never again. Not even to save my life."

"Now, darling." Emma sat down beside him. "You can reschedule your test. You can stay in bed until you start feeling better. You have another chemo treatment this afternoon. Kathy will be here around 3:00, unless…you'd rather me take you."

"I'm sure you are too busy. I'll go with Miss Kathy. I'm okay, you can go on to work."

"Well, if you're sure." Emma hesitated in the doorway and then left.

Corey collapsed on his pillow again unable to summon the energy to cry.

"Oh, Corey, dear, there's a new box of cereal in the…What's wrong, honey?" Emma opened the door and rushed to Corey's bed.

"Mom, don't leave me alone. Can you take me for treatment today? I…I just want to be with you."

Emma rocked her son in her lap as she had done when he was a baby. "Of course. I'll…well…I'll cancel my meetings today. I'll stay here and cook you a fancy breakfast, and then let's eat out for lunch before going to the hospital. Now, you get dressed while I make some phone calls and get started in the kitchen." She headed toward the door. By the way, are those the pajamas that Aunt Grace gave you last summer? I thought you hated them."

Corey looked down horrified. "Yeah, I hate these little turtles. I'm sure I didn't put this on last night."

Chapter Nineteen

"Sir Gideon? Sir? There you are." Darius rushed into the Borealis Light Bar clutching his hand-held computer. "Sir, you have three meetings scheduled this afternoon. Everyone has been trying to locate you. The Education Chairman wants to know why you didn't show up for your lecture at the Botanical Fertilization Annual Festival. The editor of the *Herald* is still waiting for your comments on the eight-day workweek proposal. The Committee for Predestination Affairs has launched an inquiry into your attempted unauthorized entry into incarnate files. And the Archangels have questions about the illegal use of your personal code for human transport. Sir? Did you hear me, sir?"

"I heard you, Darius. You really must learn to relax a little. Would you like an Illuminary? It's quite refreshing, especially with these little rainbow sprinkles." Gideon sipped at his chalice of light.

"But, sir, sales of your books are down, and the *Journal of Guardianship* canceled your column. The only thing that has gone up is your email. All of angelkind is wondering if you have really been compromised, if the great Sir Gideon has gone over the edge and, I don't know how to say this politely, become interested in an incarnate, bonded with a boy, hugged a human."

Gideon drained his chalice and stood up. "Reschedule all my appointments for tomorrow, or better yet, the day after. I need to take care of more important matters. And, Darius, get a life why don't you?"

"But, sir, you can't cancel a meeting with the Archangels. It just isn't done." Darius cringed.

"I'm not canceling. You are." He spoke his transporter code and braced himself for the jolt that never came. "Locked out of my own code? How annoying! Somebody's made a big mistake. Well, when technology fails, rely on the manual method." Gideon's wings materialized instantaneously, gleaming like iridescent opals of swirling light. He rose and then dived earthward through the field of clouds below.

Nurses raced for the crash cart. Dr. Robinson bellowed orders. An orderly lifted Corey to the waiting stretcher and began loosening his clothing. One nurse slapped an IV bag to the pole while another slipped the needle into a vein on his arm. The doctor placed an oxygen mask on the boy's face and held his stethoscope to his chest.

"Shall I get Mrs. Scott?" a nurse said.

"Yes, this might be the beginning of the end." Dr. Robinson shook his head.

Emma rushed into the hospital room. "What's happened? This is just a reaction to the medication, right? He's going to be getting better." She nodded furiously as if hoping to elicit the same response from the doctor.

"Mrs. Scott, Corey is suffering from internal bleeding. It's one of the effects of the leukemia.

Chemotherapy has only delayed this condition and given your son a few more precious months of life. There is not much we can do for him now, except to keep him comfortable and monitor his condition."

"But what about a bone marrow transplant? What about experimental treatments? There's got to be something you can do." Emma was frantic now. "He can't die! We had such a wonderful lunch together. We talked for almost an hour and had a banana split for dessert and walked to the mall and threw pennies in the fountain and…he's such a wonderful boy." Emma picked up her son's hand and held it to her lips.

The next morning, the familiar smell of antiseptic permeated the air and Corey heard the hum of a machine by his bedside. He forced open his eyes.

"Gideon?" the boy said weakly, squinting in the brightness. "Don't you come with a dimmer switch?"

The angel sat in the bedside chair reading a book he found in the drawer of the nightstand. His aura lit up the hospital room with an ethereal golden radiance.

"Oh, sorry." The radiance dimmed to a warm, comfortable glow. "How's that?"

"Better. Where's Mom?"

"She's gone to get some breakfast, finally. She stayed at your bedside all night. We weren't sure you were going to make it through." Gideon put the book on the nightstand and took Corey's hand.

"I'm dying, aren't I?" Corey turned his head and a tear wet the pillowcase.

"Yes, the doctors can't do anything else for you. The cancer is in your lymphatic system. It's too widespread even for chemotherapy or radiation treatment."

"I can't die yet, Gideon." Corey gripped the angel's hand and turned imploring eyes on him. "I just can't do it. It would be so horrible. I'm afraid."

"Corey, haven't I managed to teach you anything over all these years? You know that death is only a transition, not the end."

"It's not death that I'm afraid of. I know you'd be with me and at least I'd be free of pain. It's just that…" He dropped Gideon's hand, turned over and covered his head with the blanket.

"Corey." Gideon gently shook the immobile lump in the bed. Only his wrist with the IV drip was exposed. "Come on out. Let's talk this over. I'll tell you some more about Heaven. It's quite an amazing place. Don't be afraid. Death has already been conquered, and I'll be with you every step of the way. Corey…"

"I'll die if I have to die, but I don't want to see God!" The lump under the covers convulsed in an anguish of tears. "I'll just drift around earth as a wisp of a spirit until one day I just fade away."

"Oooh, that must have hurt." Gideon winced sarcastically. "You just had an acute attack of self-pity. In fact, I think it has reached toxic levels. Maybe I should call the doctor." Gideon uncovered the boy's face. "I thought we went over this already. Didn't you renounce evil? Didn't you ask God's forgiveness? That's all there is to it."

"But I don't feel forgiven," Corey said in a whisper and pulled the blanket back up over his face.

"Why," Gideon said to the ceiling, "do they always need some kind of special effect? It must be a TV generation thing." He shook his head. "You have to believe it first, idiot. Then forgive yourself."

"I told you. I can't, even if God ever would. I don't know what will happen after I die, but there is no way I'm going anywhere near Heaven. So maybe you had better go find someone else to guard."

"No, I'm in this for the long haul. I'll be here when the time comes. Your mom is on her way back and I have a couple of meetings to attend. When I'm gone try to accept your perfectly human mistake and get over it. God has."

Emma entered the room sipping a cup of coffee, and rushed to the bed. "Corey! You're awake! How are you feeling? Would you like something to eat?"

"No, Mom. I'm not hungry, just tired, very tired. I don't want to move or talk or think or feel. I just want to be a statue and lie here forever." Corey sighed and closed his eyes.

"Honey, I have a surprise for you. Rindy is here. She drove in early this morning after finally getting the news of your illness. We've been talking over breakfast and she wants to see you. Can I bring her in?"

Corey nodded and a young lady in a navy blue business suit entered the room.

"Rindy?" Corey asked. "You've changed."

"And you, too, little brother. How are you feeling?" She sat down on the bedside and took her brother's hand.

"Oh, I've been better. You, on the other hand, look great, very professional. What's been going on?"

"When I finally got my act together, I enrolled in a technical college and studied to be a paralegal. Now I'm working as a legal assistant at a district attorney's office. I'm doing well, and that makes this meeting even harder for me. I could have called or visited at any time. Sick or not, Corey, I should have come sooner. I guess I've been afraid of coming home. You know what an idiot I was running off with that biker trash. I should have been a better example for you. I've really failed as a sister and a daughter and I was afraid you and Mom wouldn't want me around anymore. Can you ever forgive me?" She stared at the floor.

"Forgive you? I never condemned you. How could I not want you around? Rindy, you're my sister! I love you no matter what you've done or where you've gone. Can't you understand that?" He reached up to hug her, and Rindy bent into his embrace. They held each other as two orphans in the wilderness searching for their lost childhood. "I'm so glad you're here now, Rindy. I've missed you."

Dr. Robinson came in examining a chart. A smile forced his solemn expression to lighten a little when he saw that Corey was awake.

"This must be the long lost sister," he said shaking Rindy's hand. "It's good that you've come."

"Doctor, you have to save my little brother. I've been an idiot, but he is the good one. He's got to live." Rindy said angrily and stood to face the doctor.

"Corey is a strong young man, and it is time for his family to be strong also. He needs love and prayers right now, not useless anger. Modern medicine has offered all that it can. If you look at Corey's vital signs…" He showed the chart to Rindy and Emma as they stood in a tight group at the foot of the bed.

The humming of the cardiac monitor was a soothing lullaby and the rails of Corey's hospital bed were as comforting as a baby crib. He let out a slow breath as he sank deeper than the deepest sleep, to a place beyond dreams. Even the alarm on the monitor did not disturb his gentle descent.

Chapter Twenty

Gideon stood before the ornate mirror in the wall in his office, adjusted his gleaming white tie, and puffed his pocket handkerchief. If he were to appear before the archangels, then he would jolly well do it in style. Darius smoothed a stray wrinkle from his boss's newly starched suit.

"Remember, sir, protocol demands that you wait for the archangels to initiate conversation. Be extremely polite, since they had to postpone this meeting for two days to accommodate your schedule. Be sure to wear your halo. Use your deepest bow and address them as Your Brilliance. Do not sit in their presence unless instructed to do so. If their aura changes to red, lower your voice. If it changes to…"

"Enough!" Gideon dismissed his assistant with a gesture. "If I were concerned with impressing the archangels, I would have re-read the protocols, too. You forget, this is not the first time I have been summoned to their office. I received my first Medal of Light at the hands of Sir Michael himself after I won the Battle of Paradise Path. I have since then been recognized five times for bravery, swordsmanship, scholarly excellence, purity, and overall greatness. All this talk about breaching the guardian code is nothing but Nimbus crowd gossip. And you would do well to spend less time socializing there yourself. The higher-ups probably want to recognize my innovative guardian techniques and methodologies. And it's about time, too. After all, I am the only angel visible to a human being on a daily and regular basis. Now, move aside."

Gideon left the office and stepped out onto the main lightway, a luminous and semi-transparent conveyor belt, that ran directly through downtown City of God. A glorious rainbow was just rising over the hills of clouds and a light mist sparkled in the eternal dawn. Gideon seldom traveled by lightway, but his transporter code had not yet been repaired, in spite of repeated emails to the Technology Maintenance Committee. The headquarters of the archangels was in the city's tallest building that rose gracefully above the smaller office buildings. Inside the building, Gideon passed the Office of Records, the Office of Executive Orders, the Celestial Tourism Steering Committee, the Coordinator of Worship, the Society for Heavenly Beautification, and the Director of Recreation and Retreat. He stepped into the elevator, pushed the seventh floor button, and seconds later stepped out into the gleaming hallway of Archangel Headquarters.

"This way, Sir Gideon." A young assistant briskly ushered him into a waiting room. "Their Brilliances are expecting you."

"Of course, they are. I hope you have alerted the media for the presentation. It will certainly make the six o'clock news." Gideon walked to the window and glanced at his reflection.

"Uh, I was not notified of a media event, sir. I could be wrong, but I was given to understand that an inquiry is to be made concerning your unorthodox use of celestial technology to transport incarnates and physical matter, your divulging of heavenly secrets to unauthorized entities, your flaunting of the guardian Code of Conduct against personal involvement in human affairs, and your attempted illegal entry into records of predestination. Have a nice day." The assistant retreated and closed the waiting room door.

Gideon, stunned, gripped the windowsill. The bustle of downtown below continued oblivious of the deafening beat of Gideon's heart seven floors above the street. "There's got to be a mistake. Surely a guardian of my position and greatness is exempt from the Code. Surely they're not going to charge me on some technicality. How tedious!"

A sudden high-pitched beeping sound came from a pocket monitor in Gideon's coat. He snatched it out and pushed the visual message key. A hospital monitor showed a flat line. Gideon stole a quick look at the door to the inquiry room and then waved his hand toward the window for a quick molecular rearrangement. The glass opened and Gideon's wings materialized before he had fallen even halfway toward the street.

Corey had watched the scene below him in fascination. His mother and Rindy had cried and held his lifeless body. They had knelt and prayed for his soul and for the strength to endure the loss of son and brother. Throughout the drama, Corey had hovered near a corner of the ceiling until a nurse covered his body with the bed sheet, and the chaplain ushered his family out of the room.

"Well, that's that." A voice of noble compassion spoke beside him.

Corey turned. "Gideon? You look so different, more dazzling than I could ever imagine. What happened to you?"

"I'm the same, Cor. You're the one who's changed. You are spirit now, having discarded that garment you wore in life. There is no need for radiance control or minimization of angelic effects as there was when you were still in your body. Come, let me guide you as my final official act as your guardian." He extended a hand toward Corey.

"Guide me? Where? No, not to Heaven! I told you; I can't go. And what's all this about your final act as my guardian? I still need you. You can't leave me yet."

"I may not have a choice," Gideon said sadly. "Remember that meeting with the archangels that I was supposed to attended? Well, I should have postponed it indefinitely. The Hierarchy apparently got a little…shall we say, particular about my, well…creative interpretation of the guardian Code of Conduct. I certainly didn't think my network access program could have been detected by those geeks in Celestial System Security. If the inquiry finds enough evidence of unauthorized activity, the next step is to schedule a formal hearing and possibly even a court martial. It might get a little sticky and so I need to see you safely to Heaven as soon as possible."

"They wouldn't court martial the great Sir Gideon! They just don't know you. You are the Great Guard, the Shining Sentinel, the Highest Hope for Humanity. You know all those titles you used to tell me?

Okay, I know you were exaggerating, but more important than that, you're my friend."

"Then, as your friend, trust me, and let me lead you to Heaven." Gideon took the boy's hand, but Corey pulled away. "Please, Corey, at least let me take you to the gates, and if you don't want to go in, I won't interfere. Indeed, no one in Heaven has the authority to force you to enter against your will. But we have to hurry. I'm sure my absence has been noticed by now and the City of God Serenity Enforcement officials will soon be looking for me."

"Okay, only to the gates, and only for you, Gideon." Corey clasped Gideon's hand and only a whisper of a breeze stirred the curtains in the hospital room.

Like giant columns of pure energy, the main gate of Heaven loomed before the two white-robed figures below. Only a few angels flew in or out on business and even fewer walked. As Gideon and Corey watched, an angel led a human spirit through the entrance.

"Well, this is it." Gideon said. "The Pearly Portal, the Entrance to Eternity, the Path to Paradise."

Corey felt a breeze stirring his hair and put his hand cautiously to his head. "I got my hair back?" he said in surprise. "How'd you do that?"

"I had nothing to do with it. You are in your pristine state. Whatever affected your body in life has no effect whatsoever on your soul."

"But I don't get it," he said still enjoying the feeling of running his hand through his hair.

"There's nothing to get, but if you'd rather be bald, I'm sure that can be arranged," Gideon said.

"No, I'll keep the hair, thanks." Corey stared down at the misty wisps that encircled his bare feet. "Why are we wearing these robes?" He pulled at the white cloth and glanced at Gideon.

"Well, for you white is for penitence, son."

"And for you?"

"Camouflage," Gideon said looking nervously over his shoulder. "All human beings enter Heaven in white as a sign of supplication at their Judgment Day."

"Judgment Day! Gideon, you know I can't go through with this! Does God know I'm here? You've got to hide me."

"Well, actually…" Gideon looked up and pulled the hood of his robe over his head. Two Serenity Enforcement agents flew purposefully toward the gates. "I could do with a little hiding myself. Why don't we go to my office and lay low for a while. Darius can cover for me and at least we can gain some time. What do you say? Deal?"

"Okay, but just for a little while until I can figure out a permanent hiding place outside of Heaven."

The two entered the high gate and took the back road toward the office district of the City of God to avoid the westward lightway. Gideon pointed out the sites and wonders of the great metropolis of Paradise. Angels flew by on important errands, silver glitter fell in sparkling cascades, harpists practiced songs in the light of eternity, and peace permeated every facet of the holy city.

"Here we are," Gideon said looking anxiously around and opening the door to his office. "Get inside, quickly."

When they entered, Darius stood up quickly still staring at the news monitor. "Thank Heaven you're back, sir. It's all over the news. The Serenity Officers are looking high and low…" He turned to face his boss and stood in silent disbelief.

"Now, Darius. Don't look so shocked. You can close your mouth now. Yes, this is Corey. His incarnation is over and we need a temporary sanctuary. Corey, this is my assistant, Darius."

"Pleased to meet you, Darius. Gideon has told me a lot about you. He said you were the most efficient and sensible personal assistant in the history of Heaven." Gideon rolled his eyes and Corey extended a hand toward the still-stunned angel whose boyish blush contrasted sharply with his neatly pressed suit.

"Pleased to meet you, too, Corey. Welcome to Heaven," Darius said shyly. "But am I given to assume that he is not officially a citizen of Heaven?" He looked knowingly at Gideon.

"Correct, Darius. He has not had his Judgment Day and we have agreed that he can stay here until he decides to either attend or to become… what was the phrase? 'A pathetic wisp of a spirit drifting eternally around the earth.'"

"I see, sir. And you are aware that the serenity of the archangels has become somewhat compromised since you did not meet the board of inquiry, aren't you? The tabloids have been flashing headlines such as, 'When Good Angels Go Bad,' 'The Hidden Dangers of Guardianship,' and 'The Second Great Casting Out'? You're the featured celebrity."

"Yes, well, at least I'll keep my fame. Listen, Darius, I've got to do some legal research. Make Corey comfortable and stall anyone that comes looking for us. Corey, have a seat and think about your situation. You and I have some serious talking to do and you will have to make the most important decision of you life. I'll be in my library if you need me." Gideon disappeared into his private library and closed the door.

Suddenly there was a knock on the main office door. Corey and Darius stared at each other.

"This is Serenity Enforcement. Open up."

Chapter Twenty-One

"Uh, yes? What can I do for you?" Darius opened the door a crack and peered out at the uniformed angels. Their badges gleamed with the golden S.E.A. letters.

"We are looking for Sir Gideon, the sometime guardian angel, author, and contributing columnist of the *Daily Herald*, and part-time swordsmanship instructor at the University of Heaven at Paradise. I believe this is his office?" The Serenity officer stood at precise attention.

"Yes, you are correct. But I'm afraid he is not exactly in his actual office at this present moment." Darius glanced at Corey hiding behind the door, nodding encouragingly.

"Does his assistant happen to know his current whereabouts?" One of the officers took out a pocket PC. "Is the guardian in the company of his young incarnate?"

"Well, technically, yes, you could say he is accompanied by Corey."

"Yes, Corey is the name. Please supply the address of the boy." The officer looked up expectantly.

"Oh, certainly." Darius could hardly believe his luck. He had only spoken the truth and yet revealed nothing. "The Scott family lives on 777-B Oakleaf Lane,

Sanford, Florida. Can I help you serenity officers in any other way?"

"That will be all. You've already been a great help." The officers turned abruptly and marched off. Darius leaned against the closed door for support.

"Are they gone?" Corey asked. "I didn't know Gideon was in such big trouble. Is it because of me?"

"Sir Gideon has stretched the boundaries of traditional guardian behavior, but the whole angel-human relationship was so untraditional from the very beginning. I believe you are the first and only human being to be able to see and talk to an angel other than those rare individuals given moments of inspired insight. And Gideon has become, well, very fond of you. If he has bent the rules a little, it was only out of love, and that should count for something. He's still the greatest of guardians and his record of sacrifices in the defense of Heaven and Earth is legendary." Darius seated himself on the couch next to Corey and put his head in his hands.

"Is there anything I can do to help? Gideon is my best friend," Corey said. "And…he's my hero."

"Just do whatever he tells you. That's what I always do. And do it in ultimate trust."

Gideon emerged from the library with as stack of ancient books. "These have not even been put on disk yet," he said. "There's got to be some legal precedent that would apply to my current situation. Darius, run a scan on these pages and search for key words: angelic will, creative guardianship, and angel-human relations. Corey and I have to have a long overdue discussion.

"Yes, sir. And if I might say so, Corey is a wonderful boy. The results of your guardianship of this soul should far outweigh any unorthodox methods you may have seen fit to employ in the dispensation of your sworn duties."

Gideon handed the stack of books to his departing assistant and then sat down beside Corey. "Son, you have come to the epitome of your existence, the highlight of your humanity, the culmination of your created being. Not every soul makes it this far. Believe me, I have had my failures as a guardian, although I do not make these publicly known. But you have known God's grace from your childhood. You have irrefutable knowledge of the existence of Heaven. And you have, I freely admit it, the love of one of Heaven's greatest angels. These are advantages far beyond what the average human soul can hope for. And yet, you're burdened with some kind of superiority complex by which you can't accept your own human failings. Do you think you're perfect?" Corey shook his head. "Only the perfect have no need of God's grace. But the paradox is that He gives it only to those who don't deserve it, and in greater measure to those who deserve it the least. Besides, don't forget, you're immortal now. Can you really imagine staying exactly as you are now, scared, disappointed, miserable for eternity?"

"You mean that even if I run, I can't fade away? I'll never get to be a wisp? Not even on Halloween?" Corey joked. "Lighten up, Gid. You look all solemn and serious. Hey, how do angels answer the phone? Halo. Get it? That was a joke."

"Here's one for you. If a W.I.S.P. is a Weak Ignorant Spineless Person, what is a Weak Ignorant Mousy Person?"

"That would be...a W.I.M.P." Corey looked down. "Do you think I'm a wimp, Gideon?"

"I think you have strengths you don't even know about. But what really matters is what you think about yourself."

"Okay," Corey sounded defeated. "If you think I should go to Judgment Court, I'll go, Gideon," Corey said slowly. "Darius told me to trust you, but I knew that already. I'll probably be struck by lightning and banished from Heaven. At least that will be what I deserve. Will you come with me?"

"I'll be with you as far as I am allowed. Eventually, however, you will have to be on your own in the presence of the Almighty and even I cannot lend you support there. You've made the right decision, and it's time we got started. Darius," Gideon called.

"Almost finished, sir," Darius called from the library.

"Take your time. Corey and I are off to Judgment Court. I'll just have to work on my legal defense later. Now for a little disguise…"

"No, not the cherub, Gideon!" Corey pleaded.

"And what's wrong with the cherub?" Gideon asked in mock offense. "Fine. You suggest a disguise."

"How about the beam of light? It's one of my favorites." Corey said and instantly a brilliant light beam shone beside the boy.

The pillars of the Great Hall stood in uniform perfection, unchanged since the beginning of time. The walkway led to the white marble steps like a polished river of glass. Golden archways held up a dome of dazzling brilliance, as if the sun had been turned inside out and set over the holy scene below. Corey peered out from behind one of the larger columns and watched the Heavenly Host assembling on the sides of the steps that led upward into the heart of the court. Radiant beings took their places and prepared to give homage toward the throne on the dais at the top of the steps.

"Are there always this many angels at a Judgment Court?" Corey asked in a small whisper.

"Oh, yes. Eternal worship and attendance on the Divine are what we were made for," Gideon answered. He had changed into his familiar form but now wore a robe of white light and his wings and halo were bright enough to cast Corey's shadow on the marble floor. "Dress clothes," the angel said in answer to Corey's surprised look.

"Cool," Corey said with approval.

"At some point in the proceedings, you will be called to come forth and present yourself before the thrones. Walk up the first section of steps to the first landing and then continue up to the foot of the dais. At this point you will be on your own. No angel has ever been witness to the reunion of Divine and created. Listen, the choir is singing. Court is now in session."

The sound of heavenly harps and melodic voices wove a spell of unearthly sweetness that pierced the depths of Corey's heart. He heard his name pronounced by non-human voices, making his humanity and his imperfection seem an ugly stain on the glorious scene. He held onto the great pillar and put his forehead against the smooth stone. "I shouldn't be here," he said. "I'll contaminate the purity of this place. I'm a wretched beggar that stumbled into the court of a king and none of the servants will dirty their hands to put me back outside. I'm sure they all know what I did that night in the woods."

"I thought we'd gone through this already." Gideon gripped Corey's shoulders and turned the boy to face him. "The only way to end your anguish is to go up those steps. The Heavenly Host has made a path for you. All of Heaven is holding its breath. In divine humility, even the King himself, upon whom all beings wait, waits for you. This is the hardest decision you've ever had to make. You have been called and must answer one way or another."

Corey looked back toward the open gates of the great courtyard. They beckoned him away from the trial before him.

"If you want to run, then run. It's your choice. You, at least, can still chose. No angel here will stop you. We cannot violate the primary law of Heaven and interfere with human free will. I am not allowed to drag a chosen incarnate up those steps no matter how much I want to. But maybe I can get away with giving an idiot boy a shove in the right direction."

"I know you're right, Gideon, and I'm being stupid. I know I should go up, but I just can't make my feet move. What would I say to Him?"

"Figure it out on the way. Now, move, or I really will push you." Gideon pulled Corey from behind the pillar and pointed him toward the walkway. "Please, Corey. I love you. Do this for me." The whisper was the gentlest caress.

Taking a deep breath, Corey stepped onto the walkway toward the steps. He buried his face in his hands and peered down only to see the whiteness of the steps gleaming below. He tried to block out all sight, all sound, all feeling as he ascended the steps of the court. A hush fell on the assembly. Harps fell silent as Corey proceeded. Halfway up the great stairs he came to the landing and risked a peek through the opening between his fingers. God's face shone before him in exquisite compassion and Corey's shaky resolve disappeared. He fell to his knees in outrage at the audacity of an unclean wretch daring to approach the Divine. He tried to make himself as small as possible and wished that the ground would just open up below and swallow him into oblivion.

Moments seemed like centuries until a voice of irresistible grace sounded in his mind, "Come." With the last shreds of his courage and dignity he picked himself up and climbed the last set of steps to the dais. His eyes never left the smooth marble and he knelt before the throne. Gideon's voice echoed in his memory. "Speak the word of reconciliation."

A single word formed in his soul and with the force of desperation he uttered it. "Pardon."

The silence of the hushed assembly deepened and Corey waited, suspended between hope and dread, joy and pain, longing and sadness, until the single word answer whispered celestial joy.

"Granted."

Chapter Twenty-Two

Tears burst from deep within Corey's soul as he glimpsed the depth of the love that allowed the imperfect to dare to ask for pardon at the throne of the Divine who granted mercy to a traitor. He felt inconceivable wonder flood into his small mind until he felt that he would be utterly undone. The small cannot withstand contact with infinity for long, and Corey felt that he would spend eternity in a stasis of bewilderment. Eyes closed to retain a minuscule fragment of being, Corey felt the touch of strong hands that pulled him to his feet and embraced him with the strength of a universe of universes. Only Christ knew the awesome humility of being human in the presence of God. He guided the boy to the edge of the dais and commended him to the care of the waiting angelic host.

Gideon had watched Corey ascend the marble steps and had almost rushed forth when the boy fell to his knees on the landing. Only the knowledge that ultimate redemption was offered to the penitent of free will had stayed his feet as he clutched a smooth pillar in desperate anxiety. As Corey rose and continued the ascension to the throne, Gideon watched as the brilliant mist encircled the boy. A fire of sympathetic agony burned in his angelic heart.

The official herald approached the lectern and made the proclamation. "The soul has been freed and found acceptable to enter the kingdom. Infinite is the mercy of God."

"Yes!" Gideon exclaimed. He turned to an angel standing near him. "Did you hear that? My boy made it."

"Sure, I heard it. I'm on witness duty, you know. How long do these Judgment Courts usually last? My summons only said 'Witness Duty, Daybreak, Judgment Court.' I've got to get back to my job. I'm a scribe on the staff of the Book of Life, I'll have you know. Very important business. I only hope I don't get another witness summons this year."

"How can you think of such mundane things at a time like this? My own boy has made it. And to think of all those hours, days, and years I spent molding his soul, teaching him, perfecting him. Ahh, the sweet taste of success after a job well done, if I do say so myself. Yes, I believe there will be quite a lot of publicity soon about Heaven's most successful guardian. I'll have to schedule the talk shows, the interviews, the lectures, and perhaps a documentary or two. Maybe it's time to start my autobiography. It will probably be required reading for guardian trainees. And perhaps a line of decorative posters featuring my picture and some inspirational quotes from my works…"

"You look like that Gideon fellow that was featured on the *Heaven's Most Wayward* show yesterday. Aren't you supposed to be wanted on charges of infringing the angelic Code of Conduct or Contact, or something like that?" The Book of Life angel looked at Gideon suspiciously.

"Nonsense. After my success today all charges will seem ludicrous. The life of a celebrity such as myself has no room for such trivial matters. What do you think of this title, "The Life of Gideon: Guardian Perfection," or maybe "Heaven's Best: The Angel and the Legend," or how about…"

"How about you pay attention to the court. The herald has just called your name, that is, if you really are Gideon." The scribe pointed to the lectern.

The herald spoke again. "Let Gideon approach the throne."

The court buzzed with amazement. The unprecedented calling forth of a non-incarnate at a Court of Judgment had not been witnessed since the Great Casting Out.

"Me? Why me?" Gideon looked around anxiously and the exit from the heavenly court beckoned.

"Looks like that court martial will be held after all," the scribe nodded solemnly.

Gideon took a deep breath and started up the steps, his wingtips dragging on the floor. As he approached the throne he felt a brilliant mist surround him and he entered the presence of the Divine. He saw himself a pompous fool, a court jester pretending to be great. For the first time he felt the awesome force of being in the presence of God. Like a speck of dust next to the infinite power of the sun, Gideon learned in one intensely painful lesson the meaning of humility. The best of angels, the perfect guardian, the one who had been given stewardship over creation, the one who practiced worship as an exact science, knelt in anguish and buried his face in his hands.

"I am nothing," he whispered as angelic tears fell like liquid diamonds.

A divine voice spoke within the burning of his heart. "The smallest infant on earth knows humility. Indeed, a soul cannot be born into a helpless body, suffer the frailties of human life, and endure the indignity of death without it. You have asked for free will to choose righteousness over evil. Let you heart's desire be granted, for you shall be incarnated as one of my own, whom you have so faithfully guarded. Be my son, rather than my servant, and choose well."

"Gideon, Gideon, you're not going to believe this!" Darius rushed up the golden street to meet his boss returning from Judgment Court. He clutched a set of documents and his face was flushed. "These orders just came in, and, well, I just don't get it." He looked at Gideon's face. "You okay, sir? The court martial has been canceled and you are to report to Birthing Administration tomorrow morning. But, the weird thing is that you have not even been assigned a new soul to guard. I don't get it!" Gideon continued his slow pace. "Sir, did you hear me! What's going on?"

"Well, I have been given a new assignment, of sorts," Gideon began thoughtfully. "I'm not really sure how I'm going to do this. There aren't any books written on angelic free will, but I'm …well…going to be born."

"Did you say 'born,' sir?" Darius stopped in shock, and then ran to catch up with his boss. "Do you mean actually born? As in screaming baby, runny nose, and dirty diapers?"

"The whole experience, Darius. I have been granted the free will that I have always wanted. Do you realize what this means? When I succeed in returning to Heaven after a life well-lived and choices well-made, I will be the first and only…" He paused and smiled. "Actually, I have no idea what to expect and can only hope for the wisdom to choose well. You will see me off tomorrow, won't you?"

"Next candidate," the birthing official called as he read from a list of names. "James Andrew Johnson."

A young soul stepped forward, eyes wide with nervousness and anticipation. The birthing official held a portfolio.

"Familiarize yourself with the strengths, weaknesses, talents, and gifts accorded to you for this lifetime. Meet with your guardian angel in room 389 for a 20-minute advisory council and be ready for your birth at 1:30 a.m. Next candidate." The official looked up and smiled as Gideon and Darius approached. "Congratulations, sir! The wishes of all of Paradise go with you. However, you do not have a portfolio and will have to discover your strengths, weaknesses, talents, and gifts on your own. You will meet with your guardian for a 20-minute session in room 390 and be ready for your birth at 1:31 a.m. Good luck."

"This way, sir. Your room is over here." They made their way back down the line of fidgeting birth candidates to room 390. "Probably one of my graduate students," Gideon chuckled to himself. "At least I know he is well-trained." But when Darius opened the door he froze and stared in surprise.

Corey, dressed in an immaculate white robe, looked back at this friend and shrugged. "I'm your guardian, Gid. Don't look so shocked. I'm pretty well informed on the ways of the world and quite an expert on choices, both good and bad."

The two friends embraced and Gideon said, "Corey, I'm so pleased." He patted the boy on the back. "I didn't think I would see you again until my lifetime was over. I guess an unconventional incarnation calls for an unconventional guardian. This will be even more fun that I had thought. Did you get wings?"

Corey turned around and wiggled a set of pearly white wings.

"How about the halo?" Gideon asked hopefully.

Corey pulled a golden circlet out of his robe.

"Transporter code?"

"But, of course. Already been issued and tried out." Corey smiled. "I'm so excited about this. It's going to be such great fun. Try to see me. Okay, Gideon?"

"You bet, but flash a little light now and then. And if I ignore your still small voice, then use your loud one. And be especially vigilant around my second and thirteenth years. I'm likely to do some stupid things. And feel free to make use of my library. Get Darius to look up any question you might have on human behavior. And especially, don't let the power go to your head. Remember humility."

Darius, beaming throughout the reunion, chimed in, "Yes, sir, sirs." He held the latest upgrade of the Omega series hand-held computers. "I've got all of Sir Gideon's works copied, translated, and compiled in a database using Celestial Query Language for instantaneous searches."

"Really?" Gideon took the hand held computer and tapped the screen with a finger. "Well, this is very clever. You never compiled all this for me."

"Well, sir, it's taken several years since your works are so extensive. But Corey will need them more than you would have."

"I guess you're right," Gideon said. "Now take good care of him and keep him away from that riff-raff at the Nimbus."

"Hey, you guys, relax. I think I can handle this. And, Gideon, remember to think before you act. Listen to your conscience, that's me. And especially, never doubt the infinity of God's grace. You taught me that lesson. Look, it's almost 1:30 and as my first official guardian act, I'm going to get you born on time."

"Yes sir, sirs. Right this way." Darius held the door open.

"Live birth, 1:31 am," the nurse called. "Male, APGAR score is 9, heart rate is 120, tag number 74-M." She cleaned the newborn baby as he cried, clenching his tiny fists and wrinkling his red forehead.

"What a beautiful, bouncing baby boy." An ethereal voice whispered near the nurse. "Carefully now. Gently into the incubator we go. That's a good boy. Hey, watch it! You almost bumped his head on the bed railing." Corey, as brilliant as a living moonbeam, gently stroked the few hairs on the baby's head as Darius looked over his shoulder. "That's better. Just relax. You're going to have a great life."

"So far, so good, sir. Now…, what do the words nimbus and bungee mean to you?"

The End

www.ingramcontent.com/pod-product-compliance
Lightning Source LLC
Chambersburg PA
CBHW071001120726
47910CB00004B/1328